Forty Miles
from Nowhere

Forty Miles from Nowhere

A Winter Adventure in Alaska
Sequel to *Remember the Eagle Day*

Guenn Martin

HERALD PRESS
Scottdale, Pennsylvania
Kitchener, Ontario
1986

Library of Congress Cataloging-in-Publication Data

Martin, Guenn, 1942-
  Forty miles from nowhere.

  Sequel to: Remember the eagle day.
  Summary: Melanie LaRue and her parents, accompanied by
numerous animals, spend the winter alone on an island in Cook Inlet,
Alaska, where they survive various adventures as well as the daily
routine and isolation, and come to realize the importance of having
other people around, not only for support, but for stimulation.
  [1. Alaska—Fiction.   2. Christian life—Fiction]
I. Title.   II. Title: 40 miles from nowhere.
PZ7.M36316Fo   1986   [Fic]   86-12010
ISBN 0-8361-3417-6 (pbk.)

FORTY MILES FROM NOWHERE
Copyright © 1986 by Herald Press, Scottdale, Pa. 15683
  Published simultaneously in Canada by Herald Press,
  Kitchener, Ont. N2G 4M5. All rights reserved.
Library of Congress Catalog Card Number: 86-12010
International Standard Book Number: 0-8361-3417-6
Printed in the United States of America
Design by Alice B. Shetler

91 90 89 88 87 86 10 9 8 7 6 5 4 3 2 1

To Clair
who has taught me courage
for living on my own inner island

WE DO NOT EXIST in isolation. We are part of a vast web of relationships and interrelationships which sing themselves in the ancient harmonies.... We do not love each other without changing each other. We do not observe the world around us without in some way changing it, and being changed ourselves.

—Madeleine L'Engle
And It Was Good

NO MAN IS AN ISLAND, entire of itself; every man is a piece of the continent, a part of the main; if a clod be washed away by the sea, Europe is the less, as well as if a promontory were, as well as if a manor of thy friends or of thine own were; any man's death diminishes me, because I am involved in mankind; and therefore never send to know for whom the bell tolls; it tolls for thee.

—John Donne

Chapter One

I WOKE UP at 4:30 in the morning feeling an odd mixture of sadness and excitement. This was our last fishing day of the summer, of setting nets, picking fish out of them, and taking them to the tender to sell. It was the end of playing games and having picnics with Uncle Kent and Aunt Rose and other fishing crews on the island. But I looked forward to the adventure of living on the island for a whole winter, just Mom and Dad and me and my horse, Kenai, the goats, some chickens, and my dogs and cat. Plus the ravens and weasels and other birds and animals that spend all year on Gresham Island in Cook Inlet, Alaska.

My name is Melanie Rose LaRue and I was thirteen years old that summer. My family and I are from Anchorage, Alaska. We had spent the summer on the island working at my dad's commercial salmon fishing business. (The story of my friendship with Long Jake, a hermit on the island, is told in a previous book, *Remember the Eagle Day*. Long Jake taught me a lot of what I know about wildlife.)

I am slender but not very tall, with curly light brown hair that bleaches out in the summer, and brown eyes. Dad says I'm getting pretty and sometimes when I look in the mirror I think he's right. Other times I think it's a hopeless case. I especially love animals and always seem to have a whole menagerie around.

At 4:30 in late August it was still dark and chilly enough to huddle around the wood stove with Uncle Kent and Aunt Rose while Dad fried eggs and potatoes and Mom mixed milk and poured juice. As we ate breakfast the light grew slowly outdoors, first gray and then silver. "Looks like a good day for fishing," Dad remarked.

"Yes," Uncle Kent replied. "There isn't much wind. It will be a little cold out on the water, though."

While everyone else finished their coffee or tea I put on my jacket and hurried out to feed Kenai and fill his big gal-vanized tub with water. The whole world was the cool silver of late August in Alaska. The water glimmered tarnished silver. Little wavelets reflected the pure gray silver of the overcast sky. The beach was old engraved silver and the tall dried grasses flashed silver in the breeze. Even the trees were dull dark silver. Above me pale silver sea gulls wheeled and fretted.

Kenai's corral and a snug little barn for him, the goats, and a few laying hens was the first thing we had built at the beginning of the summer in a cleared area close to our house site. Now the house was nearly finished, too. In fact, we'd be able to finish it in a week or two when the fishing season was over, and then we'd move in. The fishing cabin

8

was not warm enough for winter.

Kenai is a quarter horse gelding. He is a big horse, strawberry roan with long blond mane and tail. He has a white spot on his face and three white legs. He is beautiful and easygoing and he is my best friend.

I carried a full five-gallon bucket of water from the rain barrel at the corner of the barn to Kenai's tub and gave him some grain. I pulled a leaf of hay off the bale and put it in his feed trough. Meanwhile he followed me around, nuzzling my shoulder and nosing at my pocket to see if I had any treats for him. "Sorry, Kenai. It's too early in the morning and it's fish day. I didn't have time to grab a carrot for you this morning."

The goats were still free to roam and graze on the point and hillside, but they had heard me and came crowding around as I left Kenai. I filled their water bucket and scratched their heads as I hurried back to the fishing cabin to get into my gear. The goats straggled along behind me. "Go on, you guys," I scolded them. "We don't need your help to get our boots on."

We pulled on boots and rain gear and zipped up our life preservers. Mom gave Dad a thermos of tea and a covered peanut butter bucket with pilot bread, Snickers, and lemon drops in it. "Here's your survival pack," she smiled.

We trudged down the beach to the running line. There we gathered into a "football" huddle and Dad prayed briefly for our safety on the water.

"Let's go catch those fish," we yelled, as we all grabbed the running line and pulled in unison till the white boat touched the beach. We piled into it and Aunt Rose started the motor and drove us out to the yellow boat. Dad, Uncle Kent, and I transferred into it and I untied it from the buoy while Dad started the motor.

9

"Bye, Mom and Rose," I shouted. "Catch fish," they shouted back.

I waved as we headed out around the point and they turned toward fishing sites on the cove.

In two summers of fishing we had evolved this early morning ritual. It was sad to think that this was the last time for it until next summer. What would next summer be like, after we'd spent an entire winter living all alone on the island?

How would it feel to stay on the island without Uncle Kent and Aunt Rose? They helped provide a buffer between me and my parents. Mom and Dad are fine, but sometimes I think they forget that I'm growing up. Even though I was eager to stay on the island all winter, I felt twinges of apprehension about being with them so much without relief. I surely couldn't do it without Kenai and the other animals!

We rounded the point and headed south toward the outer beach fishing sites. The water was just choppy enough for the boat to plane well and we seemed to fly along. The world still seemed silver under the cloudy sky. The early colors of fall splashed across the dark silver bluffs, scarlet and gold and brown among the late summer silvery green leaves, a constantly changing mosaic in the morning wind.

I watched Dad drive the boat. He wore his Greek fisherman's cap. His face looked warm and kind as he squinted his eyes against the glare of the water. His lips formed a half-smile under his brown mustache and I wondered what he was thinking. I think my dad is very good-looking. Uncle Kent leaned against the opposite side of the boat from me. He wore a knit cap over his longish brown hair. His face is full and stern-looking except when

10

he smiles. Then his eyes light up and nice wrinkles form around his smile.

We pulled into the first site and I tied the end of the net to the buoy while Uncle Kent tied the cheater lines onto the other end of the net. Dad set the 210 feet of net straight and smoothly. Kent jumped out over the bow and pulled it up tight to the onshore anchor while I held the boat. All the corks floated in a straight line on top of the water from the buoy to the shore. Underneath the water, the lead line held the mesh of the net down so that fish swimming along the shore would swim right into it and get caught by the gills. In less than a minute we were on our way to the next site. Uncle Kent set that net. We made an efficient team after two summers of fishing together. At the last site Dad said, "Now it's your turn, Melanie."

I'd been hoping Dad would let me set a net on this last day. The first summer of fishing I was just a helper, but the second summer I began to learn all the aspects of fishing, including setting nets. So I took the motor while Dad tied the net to the buoy and Kent tied on the cheaters. Then I backed around carefully, watching so the line wouldn't tangle in the prop, and when I was headed toward the onshore anchor I turned up the throttle. I stood with my toes turned away from where the net rushed smoothly out over the stern so it wouldn't catch on my boots. My heart still pounded whenever I set a net because they can get all tangled up, but this one went out just right.

I slowed down as I neared the beach, then quickly cut the motor and tilted it up. Dad jumped over the bow with the cheater line and Uncle Kent leaped over the side to hold the boat. "Good set, Mel," Dad called as he pulled the net up tight, untied the cheater and coiled it. "Well, let's tie off to the buoy here and have some tea," he added.

11

"This will be a pretty slow day, I imagine. If we sit here we can watch the falcons, and maybe the oyster catchers will come over to say good-bye."

The birds are one of my favorite things about the island, especially since my friend, Long Jake, explained them to me and I later read his books about them. Early in the summer we heard a bird scolding loudly whenever we'd come to this site. One day I spotted it, flying in tight circles near the top of the bluff. A little reading in the bird book was all we needed to tell us this was a peregrine falcon scolding us for getting too near her nest high on the cliff.

Before long we could spot Mrs. P.F. or her husband scolding as soon as we pulled into the sight. I wished I could see one of them swoop for prey, but we never did. When peregrine falcons dive they reach speeds of up to 180 miles per hour. I suspect they did most of their hunting up on the mountain above the bluff. All summer long one of them always came out and scolded us, flying with quick wingbeats around the area of the nest, or soaring silently out over the water. I always thought it was Mrs. P.F. because she was so possessive about her nest, like my mom.

That last day we tied the boat on the buoy and leaned back in the bow and stern to watch the sky. Soon I saw the familiar shape of the falcon soar out over the top of the bluff. "There's one of them," I pointed, just as Kent pointed toward another one.

"Look, they're both flying!" he exclaimed. We watched as they soared and flew, high above the bluff. One flapped her wings quickly, then caught a draft and soared, suddenly flipping over, diving, doing an aerial somersault, double flipping, then swooping low over us and flapping quickly up into the air again.

They seemed to be dancing up there in the air, weaving

around each other joyously. Then suddenly there was a third falcon in the dance, this one slightly smaller and perhaps not quite so graceful, but just as joyful and free as the other two. "The baby," I breathed, as Dad and Kent and I watched in amazement. The falcon family put on a real show for us, as though they knew this was our last fishing day and wanted us to remember them all together, dancing joyfully in the sky.

Finally they flew purposefully back over the top of the bluff. "I guess they're going to teach the baby how to hunt," I said, out of a kind of daze.

"Or else they saw those fish coming and knew we'd have to get to work," Daddy replied, as corks began to bob and fish splashed and fought in the net.

"A school of silvers!" Uncle Kent exclaimed.

Silver salmon are the most fun to catch when you are sport fishing with a rod and reel because they put on a spectacular fight. They fight hard when caught in a net, too. I think silvers are the prettiest of all the salmon. They average around eight pounds and are perfectly shaped and proportioned with shining silver scales and a silver sunburst on their tails. They're good to eat, too. I like when Mom fixes a whole one with her special almond stuffing and bakes it in the oven. Plain silver steaks are good baked or grilled, too. Their flesh is paler than red salmon or king salmon meat but the flavor is delicious.

We waited until we thought most of the fish in that school were caught, then untied the boat from the buoy. We pulled the net up over the bow and across the boat and began to pull ourselves down the net, picking out the lovely silvers as they came flopping over the side. I used to feel sorry for the fish caught in our nets as they swam toward their home streams and gasping their last breaths in the bottom of our boat, but Daddy explained that they will die anyway as soon as they have spawned in the home stream or lake. If too many fish spawn in one stream or lake, the tiny baby fish don't survive because there isn't enough food to go around. Meanwhile, people all over the world need the good nourishment that salmon can provide. As long as we make sure some salmon get into the streams and spawn for future years, it's good to harvest the extras. Realizing that, I simply don't let myself think about the fish dying.

We picked through the three nets and covered the fish with wet burlap bags, then tied up to a buoy again to wait for more fish to hit. Uncle Kent talked about what he planned to do in the winter. "I'd like to buy a small plane that needs to be rebuilt and work on it when I don't have work to do for other people. Then in the spring I can sell it and make a little money on it, I hope." Kent is an airplane mechanic but he works on cars and boat engines too. I like to watch him take our boat motors apart and put them back together again so that they work properly. His hands are small for such a big person so he can handle delicate little parts quite easily. His hands are permanently black from constantly working with greasy parts and his clothes are usually oily and greasy too.

"I think you should build a little helicopter," I suggested. "Then you could come to visit us on the island this winter."

"Don't you think you'll get lonely over here with your mom and dad and Kenai and the dogs and goats and hens and cat?" Uncle Kent teased.

"I really don't know," I replied seriously. "It's hard to imagine what it will be like. After all, it's really an experiment, to see if we can do it. I like the idea of being completely independent and not having to rely on anyone else for anything. I guess I'll miss my friends from school a little, but sometimes I just get upset with them anyway. I spend an awful lot of time helping them with problems that seem pretty trivial to me."

"And we won't be completely isolated, either." Dad put in. "That's why I brought the little generator and two-way citizens band radio. I plan to call Anne's dad on a regular schedule to let him know how things are going. The only time we might have trouble getting through is in a severe storm and that's not likely to happen often."

Frankly, I envy you, being able to do this," Kent said. "But I couldn't very well fix airplanes on Gresham Island."

"Yes, we are fortunate to be able to do this. With Anne being a writer and me able to get a sabbatical to do some writing, too, we have the ideal situation, if Melanie can manage with her schoolwork. And it *is* an experiment. If we can't stand it, we can always leave."

"Could we get a helicopter big enough to haul Kenai?" I asked, knowing we really didn't intend to leave.

Kent laughed. "Sure you can, if you can persuade him to board it. But I don't think you'll decide to leave. I wish I could stay to help you finish the house, but I need to get back to mechanicking if I want to have any business."

"Right now my biggest concern is where we'll get water if it freezes before there's enough snow to melt."

"Well, if worse comes to worst, we can use Long Jake's spring," I said. "He said it never freezes until the middle of winter. By then we'll have plenty of snow. It would be a long way away, I know, but we do have the cart and tanks so Kenai could pull it."

I still could not think of Long Jake without a pang of pain. Long Jake was the old man who had owned the island and lived on it with his goats in complete isolation for many years. When we had come to fish on the island the previous summer I had managed to make friends with Long Jake and learned to love him dearly. We all looked forward to this winter when we would be on the island with him and he could learn to know Kenai and could teach me out of his vast knowledge of birds and animals on the island. But Long Jake died before we returned to the island, before he ever got to meet Kenai, and I could hardly bear it. Now Long Jake's cabin high up in the hills, his goats, and the whole north end of the island belonged to me, but I would much rather have had Long Jake himself to share the coming winter.

"That would be a worst," Dad smiled. "It would be quite a job to haul enough water down the hill, even with the cart." We had, with Uncle Kent's help, devised a two-wheeled cart with wide beach buggy tires and two big covered tanks on top. On a trip back to Anchorage during the summer Dad had found a harness for Kenai. Now, with me leading him, he hauled our water about a half mile from the waterfall to the fishing cabin. The harness came in handy, too, for pulling firewood up the beach after bringing it from the mainland in our boats. We also used the cart to haul building materials to the house site. Kenai was a workhorse as well as a pleasure horse and I felt proud of him.

The lovely silver day drifted by. We took our fish to the holding boat at lunchtime and had vegetable soup and corn muffins for lunch. Then we went back to the outer beach and set the nets out for low tide. The tide in Cook Inlet changes as much as 24 feet in six hours, so we must set our nets in deeper water for low tide or they will go dry. You can't catch fish in dry nets!

Since the tide wouldn't be high enough to set the nets back in before closing time, we took all the lines off the onshore anchors, which were really rocks with bolts and a link of chain in them. Mom, Dad, and I would pull the outer anchors and buoys by ourselves the next day, since Uncle Kent and Aunt Rose were going to leave on the tender. As the afternoon hurried by I felt sad about having them leave. Uncle Kent is always good at making me feel better when I'm in a grumpy mood. He says something "punny" and I end up laughing in spite of myself. He gets into grumpy moods himself sometimes so he understands how I feel and that the only way to get through to me is by making me laugh.

Uncle Kent and Aunt Rose are my mother's youngest brother and sister. They are so much younger than my mother that in a lot of ways they seem more like my older brother and sister. Aunt Rose is only eight years older than I am. She and I enjoyed each other all summer. We mended nets together and I taught her how to ride Kenai. We took long walks on the beach or up the hill to the little spruce grove where Long Jake is buried. We talked a lot about what we were going to do after we finished school— of course, she is in college and majoring in anthropology, so she has a better idea of what she is going to do than I have. But I would like to go to an equestrian school so I can learn to work with horses.

I tell Rose things I really couldn't tell my mom, like that I sort of liked Jim Hanson, who fished with his family on the other side of the point, but not enough to get as serious as he seemed to want to get. I mean, I enjoyed talking with him and singing while he played guitar and stuff, but I wasn't ready to be kissed or even hold hands. Most of my friends back in Anchorage would have loved it, but I just didn't feel like kissing, at least not with Jim Hanson.

I could tell all this to Aunt Rose, and we laughed about it—but she understood, and we decided we didn't need to be in any hurry to get married. There were so many things we wanted to do first. Rose wanted to travel. I wished I were older so I could go with her.

The calm, silvery afternoon ended even though I didn't want it to. We picked the fish out of our nets and I moved them to one side while we pulled the nets, stacking them carefully in our boat. Some fishing people put their nets in bags, but we like to stack ours in the open boat, where they dry out more easily, and we think they are easier to set. We delivered the fish to the tender; Mom and Rose had taken Rose and Kent's things to the tender earlier in the afternoon.

At the cabin Mom was making sandwiches for them to eat on the noisy, smelly all-night trip back to Kenai. Kent and Rose changed out of their fishing clothes and disappeared one at a time into the little sauna where they could shower with the garden sprayer. I saddled up Kenai and got his harness ready. Then I rode him around the point to the Hansons' camp while Dad took Rose and Kent around in the boat. Hansons had delivered all their gear to the tender, too, and Kenai and I were going to help them pull their boats up the beach. Then Dad would take them out to the tender with Kent and Rose.

Hansons' house was all boarded up and already looked deserted. I felt a twinge of loneliness thinking that it would be like that all winter. I was so used to riding Kenai over in the evening and finding Jim and Rob mending nets or singing with the guitar or jogging down the beach to the rope swing on a big cottonwood. Mrs. Hanson didn't help fish like Mom, but she kept busy baking goodies for her hungry family and she did beautiful needlework, mostly things that she designed herself. On nice evenings when I came by she would be sitting in her favorite lawn chair in the evening sun stitching away.

This evening, though, the lawn chairs were all stored away. Rob was coiling up the running line. Jim had just run the two boats up onto the shore as far as they would go and was helping his father carry the motors up to their gear shed. Mrs. Hanson walked over to greet me as I dismounted, took Kenai's saddle off, and began to put on his harness.

"Well, Melanie, do you really think you can make it through the winter here without any other young people around?" she asked.

"Oh, you know my animals are my best friends anyway," I laughed. "And I'll have them with me. I'm looking forward to being independent." I finished fastening the harness and led Kenai down the beach to where Jim had ropes ready to tie onto it. Dad and Kent and Rose drove up in our boat and jumped out to help. Everyone pushed on the stern of the boat while I went to Kenai's head and talking to him quietly.

"Okay, boy, let's go now." Kenai lunged forward. Once the boat started moving it pulled easily over the gravelly beach to its winter resting place up near the cabin. I unhitched Kenai and everyone worked together to tip the boat on its side and turn it over. In no time at all the second boat was ready for winter. Then it was time to say goodbye.

I shook hands all around with the Hansons, giving Mrs. Hanson a hug. I was glad that Jim wouldn't try to kiss me with so many people around. "I'll miss you," I told him honestly. "I hope you have a good year in school."

"Well, I personally don't envy you, having to do school-work on your own," he said. "But you'll probably manage. You seem to be good at that. Take good care of Kenai." He grinned and mischief shone in his eyes: "Whenever you get lonely this winter, just remember I'll be back next summer."

"Oh, I'll remember—with fear and trembling!" Then it was time to say good-bye to Kent and Rose, and that was harder. I hugged Aunt Rose tightly. "Have a good year," I whispered; that's all I could say without tears sliding out of my eyes.

She hugged me back and didn't say a word; it was all in her eyes that she would miss me and the island and that I was to take good care. "I love you, Mel."

Uncle Kent gave me a great big bear hug. He is sort of like a big teddy bear anyway. "Well, Melly, by the time we get to Kenai I'll probably be completely tenderized. Don't you envy us, getting to ride on the tender?"

"That's one thing that makes me glad I'm staying here," I laughed. "Too bad Uncle Greg couldn't come after you in the plane."

"Well, when I get home I'll have the Champ available. Maybe I'll fly over and check on you every once in a while before freeze-up. You'd better be doing your schoolwork or I'll report you to the school board and they'll come and get you!"

They all climbed into our boat and pushed off. Dad called, "Better head home right away, Melanie. Mom will have dinner ready." Kenai and I stood and watched them go, then I turned to him and began to unbuckle his harness.

"Well, we're on our own now, boy. I wish we could ride up the hill to Long Jake's cabin and on up to the spruce grove, but I guess that will have to wait. After dinner there's a lot of work to do. Oh, Kenai, we'll have so much fun this winter, just you and me!"

Then, in the middle of my excitement I thought, "But I *do* wish Long Jake were alive."

I cinched up the saddle girth and mounted Kenai. We walked slowly down the beach toward the point. The Hansons and Kent and Rose were climbing aboard the tender. The breeze had died and the silver water was perfectly calm, reflecting the silver sky. Between the sky and the water the dark mountains rose, calm and implacable. They seemed so strong, so permanent, completely immovable in the middle of the changing world. I knew they weren't; I had seen a huge avalanche near one of our fishing sites during the summer. Part of the island just peeled off and slid into the sea, causing a great cloud of dust and a huge wave that moved outward into the inlet. When the dust had blown away, there was a patch of bare rock, harsh and angry, and at its foot a pile of sharp-edged boulders, some as big as houses. So even the hills could be shaken, though tonight in the calm, silver air, with everyone but the three LaRues going away for nine months, the mountains seemed very peaceful and forever.

By the time Kenai and I had walked slowly around the point, Dad had returned and tied up the boat and the tender was chugging out into the inlet, too far away for us to see the people on board.

I put away the saddle and harness, settled Kenai in his corral, and fed him and the goats and chickens in a kind of daze. I couldn't decide whether to feel happy or scared or sad. The enormous reality of what we were planning to do settled into me. When I walked back to the fishing cabin I could see that it was just settling into Mom and Dad too.

Dad stood at the door gazing off over the inlet toward the little speck on the horizon that was all we could see of the tender. Mom quietly and deliberately put the food on the table: baked silver salmon steaks, coleslaw made from fresh cabbage from our own garden, and savory rice.

Mom has curly brown hair, too, but hers is permed. She wears glasses, has a double chin, and her teeth stick out a little, but she's my mom. Her face is almost always smiling and that's good because she looks lifeless when she isn't smiling.

"Dinner's ready," she said. We sat down at the table which seemed empty without Rose and Kent. We reached out automatically to join hands for prayer. But Daddy didn't pray right away. Instead he said, "Well, girls, this is it. We're on our own."

"Yes," Mom agreed. "And after all our planning and anticipation I don't know whether to laugh or cry or be scared to death."

"Why, that's just how I feel!" I exclaimed, relieved. "I was telling Kenai I had no idea I would feel so mixed-up about being left here alone. We've looked forward to this as an exciting adventure all along and now all of a sudden it's not just a plan, it's really happening and. . . ." I trailed off.

"I think it's perfectly normal to have ambivalent feelings about anything new and unknown," Daddy said. "Robert Frost says it well in 'The Road Not Taken.' Well, we've passed the fork in the road now, and started down the one road, so we might as well make the most of it." He lifted his water glass and smiled. "Here's to a good winter on Gresham Island!"

Mom and I lifted our glasses and touched his. "Cheers!" we said as we all laughed and drank.

Then we joined hands again and Daddy prayed, "Father, we thank you for this coming nine months on the island and we give it all to you. May this be a time for us all to grow in our knowledge of ourselves and each other and you. Bless the work we have come here to do and make it useful for your purpose. We ask that you give the tender safe passage to Kenai, and we thank you for this good food. Amen."

As soon as we had eaten, it was high tide—so we hurried out to pull the nets up onto the mending racks. We planned to mend them before hanging them in the gear shed for the winter. All the spare nets had already been mended and put away. It had been such a calm, easy day there wasn't much mending to be done and Dad said we should have them all in the gear shed by noon the next day. We pulled up the last one as the sun sank over the mountains on the mainland and Mom said, "Melanie, you don't have to help with the dishes tonight. I'll do them and you can have some free time."

I smiled at her gratefully, "Thanks, Mom," and walked up the beach to one of my favorite sitting logs on the point. From this log I could gaze out across the inlet toward the far purple line of the Kenai mountains on the other side. Or I could look across the channel toward the great masses of the Chignik Mountains rising almost straight up from the water, first dark purple, then silver purple, and finally the high silver snow peaks against the lavender sky. I could even turn around and gaze up along the green ridges to the top of the mountain on Gresham Island. The air was so still that the only movement of the water was the tide ebbing in a barely detectable current.

I can't imagine living for long away from the mountains and the sea. Whenever my life gets cluttered and complicated and churned up, if I slip away to where I can gaze at the mountains and feel the regular rhythm of the waves breaking against the shore, things begin to come back into perspective for me again. My heartbeat slows down to match the sea rhythm; all the clutter and clatter drops away in the calm presence of the mountains. That night I thought of one of my favorite poems by Emily Dickinson:

> The mountains grow unnoticed—
> Their purple figures rise
> Without attempt, exhaustion,
> Assistance, or applause.
>
> In their eternal faces
> The Sun, with just delight
> Looks long, and at last and golden
> For fellowship at night.

I looked long at the mountains and slowly my mixed-up feelings of grief and fear and eagerness resolved themselves into a sense of peace and contentment. I knew everything was going to be all right.

Chapter Two

WE HAD STORED all our furniture and other supplies that needed to be kept dry in the gear shed during the summer while the fishing equipment was being used. Before they left, Kent and Rose helped us move all those things into the new house, where we stacked it in the kitchen, which was finished. Uncle Kent helped Dad install the big black wood heating stove in the living area, and the shining black and white oil range in the kitchen. The tender brought a whole winter's supply of oil for the range in fifty-five gallon drums. We rolled them up the hill and set them just outside the kitchen where Daddy could pump the oil into a tank set on a frame outside the kitchen wall. Mom and Dad had decided that we should completely finish the house before moving in. There were still many shelves to put up and the bed platforms to build upstairs.

But before we worked on the house we had to put away the fishing gear. So the day after Kent and Rose left we worked very hard. All three of us went out in the yellow boat to pull the anchors. Catching the buoy, we pulled the rope up as far as we could, then Dad hooked it around the post in the stern of the boat and started the motor. At full power the motor ground away and we didn't seem to be going anywhere until we felt a soft jerk as the anchor pulled out of the mud. Dad stopped the motor and we all pulled hand over hand until the big heavy anchor banged against the side of the boat and, exhausted, we hauled it in over the side. It took us two hours to pull nine anchors. The other buoys were attached to metal stakes we had driven in the mud at low tide. The stakes would stay all winter, so we just detached the buoys and left the ropes to sink. In the spring we would find them again at low tide.

With a boat full of anchors and buoys we headed back to the cabin. We tied the boat to the running line to be un-loaded at high tide, then quickly mended the nets we had used the day before. I should say, Mom mended them. Dad and I worked away at it, but Mom had mended three medium-sized holes before we had finished our small ones. She said practice makes perfect, but my fingers all turn to thumbs when I'm mending nets and I get mixed up about where I'm supposed to hook onto the edges of the tear. Dad just plain doesn't like to mend nets. He usually finds something urgent to do when nets need to be mended. Mom and Aunt Rose and Uncle Kent all seem to enjoy the task, especially if the weather is good. They take their mugs of coffee and the radio and talk and laugh and sing while they work. I want to learn to be a good net mender so I can be in on that fun.

Anyway, the nets were mended quickly because they

had few holes. We tied up each one, put it in the cart, and pushed it up to the gear shed. Gill nets are heavy, not only because of the amount of material in them, but because of the heavy leadline attached to the lower edge to keep the net hanging vertically in the water. Dad stood on a step stool in the gear shed and tied each net to the rafters while Mom and I stood underneath straining to hold up masses of webbing and corks. We wondered what our friends back in Anchorage would think if they saw us struggling to hold up the nets, with corks bobbing around our legs like hula skirts and our feet tangled up in leadlines. We started giggling at how funny we looked. We laughed so hard we didn't have the strength to hold up the net and Dad got stern with us.

"Now ladies, settle down," he admonished us, but the corners of his mouth turned up and he laughed too.

"I think we need a little snack," Mom breathed between giggles. "Then maybe we can get serious and work properly."

Dad and I made space for the rest of the nets while she went into the cabin. Soon she came back with a plate of pilot bread spread with peanut butter and honey and cups of milk. We sat on a log on the beach and snacked.

"I feel all light and happy," I announced. "Maybe it's laughing gas. But really I think it's just because I feel good. It's a lovely sunshiny day, this is a beautiful place, and we are all working together. It's fun to work together like this."

"I agree," Mom said. "There's something about working hard together that lifts the spirit. I not only feel strong and capable but full of vitality and zest for living. I always feel that way on bright fall days, but especially when I'm working or playing with you. This is fun!"

Dad laughed. "It's only fun because you are doing all the giggling and I'm doing all the work," he teased. "Well, maybe if you develop enough laughing gas *that* will hold the nets high enough so that I can tie them up. Come on, we have only three more."

We finished hanging nets and then I went after Kenai to help us haul the anchors and buoys up in the cart. He snorted at me as I walked up to the corral and the goats gathered around hopefully. "Hi," I told them, hugging Kenai's neck and scratching heads all around. "Want to help with the work?" I put Kenai's harness on him and led him out, leaving the gate open so the goats could go out and graze. I led Kenai down the beach to where Mom and Dad had piled half the anchors in the cart and hitched him to it. In no time at all we had all the anchors and buoys stacked in the gear shed and Kenai had helped! I felt like I could just bubble up and float away into the large blue sky.

"Mom, may I ride Kenai while you get lunch?" I asked. "I will do the dishes afterward. I feel like I *have* to ride."

"Of course," Mom smiled. "Have fun. Lunch will be ready in half an hour."

I put away Kenai's harness and put the bareback pad on him. I let the dogs loose so they could run with us. Talkeetna is a white Siberian husky with blue eyes. Goofus, her pup, is all legs and big erect ears, gray and tan and brown-eyed. I let Kenai have his head up the beach toward the point. Goofus and Talkeetna ran flying behind us, stretching their legs. The wind streamed through my hair and Kenai's mane as he settled into a smooth canter. It felt like flying. We rounded the point and pounded down the beach to the rocks past the boarded-up Hanson cabin. There I pulled Kenai to a stop and leaned on his neck, breathing heavily, until the dogs caught up. They ran as hard as they could until they reached us and dropped to the ground panting.

"You sillies," I laughed at them. "You wouldn't have to run so hard. We always stop eventually." They lay there breathing heavily with their pink tongues hanging out and big grins on their faces. They were happy.

The sun came out from behind a cloud and suddenly the whole landscape was bright. The water shimmered gold and silver, the dry grasses along the beach turned to gold, and the leaves on the cottonwood trees fluttered in a mosaic of bright yellow, dark gold, dusty green, and brown. Cloud shadows lay in purple patches on the mountains across the channel, changing their shapes in a kind of giant puzzle. A long line of white-winged scoters flew from east to west just above the surface of the water.

It seemed to me that I could not fully *feel* the beauty, joy, and peace that came from both inside and outside of me. It was all too grand for one small person. I sat on Kenai's back for ten minutes, trying to absorb this feeling into my memory. I had learned after Long Jake died that it's good to have memories of special times and feelings, so I consciously tried to experience times like these fully so they could always be mine.

Finally I told Kenai, "Well, we'd better get back now. Mom will have lunch ready and there's lots of work to do this afternoon." We walked home. Kenai paced slowly along, rather dignified, while I sat loosely on his back. The dogs stopped to sniff and explore every log and piece of driftwood on the beach, then hurried to catch up with us again.

With the fishing gear all stowed in the gear shed, we were free to work on the house. All afternoon Mom measured the places for the shelves in the pantry, Dad cut the boards to fit, and I sanded them enough to prevent us from getting splinters. We all worked together to put them up. While we worked we sang, discussed all kinds of things from the best way to store flour through the winter to which birds might winter on the island with us, and muttered when the saw slipped or a nail bent under the inaccurate pounds of the hammer.

It took us five more days to finish all the shelves and build the bed platforms, interrupted by necessities like hauling water, baking bread, and riding Kenai.

On Sunday we took the day off. Since the tide was especially low we took a boat across to the sandbar at the mouth of the river and dug for razor clams. Razor clams are found in sandy beaches that are covered with water at high tide. When the tide goes out they stay just under the surface, and a telltale dimple forms in the sand above them. We slide the clam shovel into the sand close to the dimple and quickly dig up a couple of shovelsful, then reach swiftly into the watery sand and grab the clam before it digs itself out of reach. Razor clams can dig themselves down into the sand very fast. An elongated oval in shape, their thin golden shells have sharp edges when they break. They are delicious to eat, fried by themselves or in chowder or white spaghetti sauce. We dug a bucketful and took them home. The weather was warm for late August, though not hot, so we cleaned them on the beach. That evening we had one of my favorite meals, little pasta seashells with white clam sauce, and we canned six pints of clams to use in the winter.

The following Friday we moved into our brand-new house. We packed all the eating and cooking utensils and leftover food from the fishing cabin the night before and carried the boxes to the new house. Dad lighted the oil range, so when we got up in the morning we had breakfast in the new house. It took all day to unpack food and store it on the shelves in the pantry, unpack books and a few knicknacks and put them on shelves, put everything away in the kitchen cupboards, and hang our clothes in the bedroom closets or put them on shelves in the bedrooms. It wasn't hard to arrange furniture because there wasn't much, and we had planned where it would be when we designed the house.

It was a snug, cozy house. It already felt like home when we sat down to eat dinner that evening. The downstairs was twenty-four feet square. The upstairs was only half that size. The front of the house, facing the cove, was one story, with a shed roof that slanted to the second story at the back of the house. The second story roof sloped down away from the cove.

We entered the house through a long narrow closed-in porch on the north side. The porch was a good place to stack wood for the heater, as well as a few tools and the gas washing machine. The rug Mom put inside the door was meant to keep mud and melted snow from being tracked into the house. Of course, she put another rug just inside the inner door, which opened into a long narrow hallway. At the back of the hallway we turned left to go up the stairs to the bedrooms. One wall of the hallway was covered with hooks for coats and bins and shelves for scarves and caps and mittens. We could sit on a narrow bench opposite to put on boots or take them off and store them underneath. On the wall just opposite the door as we walked in, Mom positioned a large patchwork wall hanging in bright colors of red, orange, and yellow.

If we turned to the left inside the front door, the hallway opened into the living area of the house. Four windows across the front of the house overlooked the cove, and a large window to the south caught some of the scarce winter sunshine. We divided the living area into two parts. The sofa, Dad's reclining chair, and Mom's oak rocker were grouped around the wood heating stove, which stood near the front wall between two windows. Mom had brightened the old brown sofa with orange, yellow, and red print pillows and put down a large braided rug. She used several weathered driftwood stumps for occasional tables. The other half of the living area had a desk-high counter under the other two front windows, slanted across the corner, and continued under the large south window. Several two-drawer filing cabinets provided storage under the counter and shelves full of books stretched from counter to ceiling between the windows. A chair for each of us completed that area. It was our work area, where I could do my school assignments and Mom and Dad could write and study. Mom had found a standard manual typewriter that was still in good shape, but she was a bit leery about whether she would be able to use it after typing on a correcting electric typewriter for so long.

Between the hallway and the kitchen were the pantry which was under and beside the stairs, and the bathroom which formed an eight-foot long inner wall for the living area. Mom put a number of our favorite bird prints and photographs on that wall. The door of the bathroom opened toward the kitchen in the southwest corner of the house.

The kitchen, work area, and the living area formed an L-shape around the walls of the bathroom and pantry. The kitchen counter and cupboards stretched twelve feet along the back wall of the house, with a narrow window above the sink through which I could see the barn and Kenai's corral. Between two windows on the south side of the kitchen stood the big black-and-white oil range, with its smooth top and high back with a warming shelf.

The pantry door was a heavy quilted curtain; against the wall between it and the bathroom door stood the freshly painted fifty-five gallon drum that was our water barrel. Our small dining table was set in the open spot between the kitchen and the work area. Under one of the south windows Mom had a shelf of ivy and philodendron and she hung a big healthy spider plant from the ceiling. She had nurtured the plants in the fishing cabin all summer and now they added a homey feeling to our new house. She hung a mixture of decorative and useful baskets, pans, and kitchen utensils on the pantry wall, and a bright Lavalee poster above the water barrel.

In our bathroom we had a compost toilet which doesn't use water for flushing and has no odor. In a compost toilet, bacteria break everything down and decompose it, leaving a small residue which is removed about once a year. Temperatures must be kept at a certain level for the bacteria to work. We provided that with a single electric light bulb which ran off the battery we used for the CB radio. The bathroom also had a sink with a large bucket underneath for waste water to be carried out. We stepped up into the shower (our good old two gallon garden sprayer) so that a bucket could be placed under the floor drain and easily emptied.

The pantry was full of shelves from floor to ceiling, with space under the stairway for extra bags of flour and other staples. The shelves were stacked high with canned goods of all kinds, dried fruits, beans and pasta, cereal and crackers. It felt good to see all that food stacked there.

We sat at the dinner table and looked around at the snug

little house. I had some of my little pig figurines on the shelves above my desk, and my favorite books, as well as some I'd never read before. Mom's Hummel goose girl figurine stood in a corner of her desk area, and Dad had a colorful papier mâché clown sitting on one of his shelves with one leg hanging over the edge. These familiar things that had made our house in Anchorage seem like home now gave continuity to our home on Gresham Island. We drank our tea from pottery mugs made by a friend in Anchorage; the chairs and sofa in the living room had been in our houses for as long as I could remember. We basked in the warmth of the shelter around us.

"Our next big task is to get enough wood to last the winter," Dad said. "I believe we'll do well to establish a routine. We'll spend the mornings working at our desks. We can each accomplish a lot if we work from 8:30 to 12:00 each day. Melanie, I believe you can easily do most of your schoolwork in that time, and that's already your writing schedule, Anne. After lunch we'll do the chores that are part of our survival here, like carrying in wood, cutting and splitting it, and packing it into the woodbox, going for water, washing clothes, baking bread, caring for the livestock, cleaning the house, and so forth. We'll try to reserve evenings for reading and playing games together. When we don't have a lot of chores to do we can go for walks or other expeditions. Sometimes we may each have separate things we want to do in that time. How does that sound?"

"That's fine with me," Mom replied. "I envision using some winter afternoons for sewing and craft-type work. That should work out well."

"It's good for me too," I said. "I want plenty of time to enjoy Kenai and the goats, and I'd like to spend an occa-

34

sional day or afternoon up in Long Jake's cabin. I think it would be neat if I could stay there for several days some time, to see if I can manage on my own."

"I'm sure that can be worked out," Dad responded. "Well, what do you say we start with writing and school-work Monday morning? Tomorrow is Saturday. We'll fill the water barrel and generally get squared away so that we can spend the afternoons next week gathering wood on the mainland. The tide will be high in the evenings for a while, and that means we can wade in over the flats with a long rope for the boat, cut our wood, and load it just before high tide, then bring it home and unload it shortly after high tide."

We cleared the table and Mom washed the dishes while Dad and I dried. Then Mom and Dad took a walk around the cove while I went out to feed and water Kenai and the goats, chickens, and dogs. We had a second fifty-five gallon drum sitting in the barn for a water barrel. Dad spent a long time trying to figure out a way to keep it from freezing in the winter. He had decided to keep a small kerosene heater beside it in an enclosed space where the heat would be kept in and the animals wouldn't be able to get to it. It would have to be warm enough to melt the blocks of snow we planned to use for water in the winter after the waterfall froze.

The barn was the first thing we had built at the beginning of the summer. It had a gambrel roof and a loft inside where the bags of feed were stacked out of harm's way. There was a regular size door in the north end. Just inside it was the space for the water barrel on one side and a milking stand for the goats on the other side. Against the wall a ladder led up to a hole in the floor of the loft, and below it covered garbage cans full of feed were arranged for each kind of animal. All of this was walled off from the livestock area. Through a door in this wall was an indoor area for the chickens with a little door in the wall at ground level where they could go out into their wire-covered pen. We had put chicken wire a foot into the ground (to help discourage the weasels from going after our chickens) and over the top of the pen (to keep out the eagles and hawks). Inside the barn the chicken pen was also well fenced to keep out weasels and martens or other small predators. But there was space for the chickens to roost up high and they seemed happy in their snug world. In the winter the heat from the kerosene heater by the water barrel just on the other side of the wall, as well as the body heat from Kenai and the goats, would help keep the chickens warm. Kenai's stall was just beyond the chicken pen. He had a big door through which he could go out into the corral. The goats shared a large stall across a narrow aisle from Kenai and the chickens, and they too had a door to the corral through the south wall of the barn.

Outside the barn, with the doors facing south, were Goofus' and Talkeetna's houses. We kept the huskies tied there most of the time, but they were allowed to run free when someone was out to keep an eye on them. We didn't want them to run off and get caught by the tide in a steep-sided cove. The cold and the current would almost certainly be too much for them to handle if they tried to swim to safety. My beige cat, k.c., had learned to love the island over the summer. He spent most of his time outdoors, and caught lots of mice, voles, and shrews. We figured he would become a mostly indoor cat again when the weather turned cold.

I didn't give the goats much to eat because they were still grazing in the woods and on the point. Kenai grazed a little, too, but he depended mainly on the feed and a little hay I gave him each day. The chickens were glad for their grain. I filled tubs of water for Kenai and the goats, gave the chickens their water, and took food and water to Goofus and Talkie. Goofus strained at his chain, crying with excitement over being fed once again, but Talkeetna stood still, trembling slightly, as I brought her food. She dug right into it; she was just as hungry as Goofus.

Feeding the animals every morning and evening would be my chore all winter. I knew that it wouldn't always be so much fun, especially when the temperature was down to -20° and the wind was howling, or when freezing rain swirled out of the woods and around the barn, turning the path into a treacherous stream of ice. But I loved the animals and I always enjoyed talking to them and petting each one.

We had been too busy to milk the goats over the summer so we let them go dry, but we planned to start milking again when the does had their kids. The chickens were meant to provide fresh eggs. I hoped they would keep laying a few eggs, at least, or they might end up in the pot themselves, and I had become friends with them. I don't believe in dining on friends.

After he'd finished eating I rode Kenai around the cove to meet Mom and Dad. The dogs trailed along behind. When I met Mom and Dad I dismounted and led Kenai so we could walk back together. Up on the bank among the thin trees we could just see our little house, all new yellow wood, in the late evening light. As we walked quietly I suddenly thought, "There is no one else around. We are completely on our own. We have to fend for ourselves, and we have to do it well."

Aloud, I said, "We can do it. We can live on this island

all winter and manage by ourselves. We're strong and capable."

"Yes," Daddy must have been thinking the same kinds of thoughts as I was. "There is our sturdy house, full of food. Let the cold winds blow. The three of us will be tucked in safe and warm, snug as three bugs in a rug."

"Well, Daddy, actually there are twenty-four of us, counting 12 chickens, five goats, Kenai, Goofus, Talkeetna, and k.c. We're a large population."

"When you put it that way, you're right," Daddy laughed. "I wonder how we are going to keep so many happy for nine long months."

"What I'm enjoying is not having any outside obligations, no phone calls, no committee meetings, no concerts to go to—although I'll probably miss the music," Mom spoke dreamily. "I'm glad we have the radio and plenty of batteries. At least we can listen to whatever they play for us on the Kenai radio station." She shook herself slightly and smiled at Dad and me, "Do you think I'm being selfish?"

Nobody answered. Was it selfish, I wondered, to want to be independent, to manage on your own, to be free of social or business obligations to other people and phone calls and interruptions and all the people and things that seemed to take up so much time and space in town? I felt sure of one thing: we *could* manage very well by ourselves. I was sure that Mom and Daddy felt that same way, too.

Chapter Three

THE NEXT MORNING while I fed the livestock, Dad talked to Grandpa on the CB, their regular weekly contact. Grandpa was glad to hear we were moved into our house. He said Aunt Rose had left for college the day before and Uncle Kent was finding plenty of work fixing sick airplanes.

As I walked back into the house I heard Grandpa's voice saying, "Be careful and God bless you. We'll talk to you next Saturday at the same time. Cottonwood Cache over." Cottonwood Cache is the name Grandpa and Grandma gave their little house, which is snuggled among a grove of cottonwood trees on the hillside.

"Gresham Island over," Dad said into the mike, and clicked off the CB. "We need to name this little house. Then that could be our CB handle," he smiled at Mom.

"You're right," Mom replied. "I wonder what it could be. This house is a shelter, it's warm and cozy, and it's very isolated. It seems like we should think of a name that reflects all that."

We began to mull over a name for our home, but it was hard to come up with anything just right. I thought about places in some of my favorite books like *Watership Down*. The rabbit warren there was a good shelter but it was high on a hill, and that didn't seem appropriate for our house on the cove. Rivendell in *The Lord of the Rings* was a safe retreat and a refuge but it was the last homely house before the mountains, and it was surrounded by a ring of magic. Somehow that didn't seem right either. One of the places in Hobbit land would be better, because hobbits relied on their own ingenuity and were quite independent. But "Underhill" wouldn't really work unless we had an earth sheltered house. I thought of Merry's home near the edge of the woods, "Brandybuck Manor," but that seemed a little too grand.

Then Mom said, "What about 'The Snuggery'? That implies that it's a cozy place where people feel close and warm."

"Oh, I like it!" I exclaimed. "It sounds just right to me."

"Sounds good to me, too," Daddy said. "The Snuggery it will be. I'll carve a little plaque with 'The Snuggery' on it to go above the door."

On Sunday we climbed the hill past Long Jake's cabin, past the grove of trees where he was buried, and on up to where there was no path. We kept climbing until it got pretty steep and Mom said she was beginning to feel vertigo. So we stopped and sat on the edge of a little cliff. Far below us we could see the whole north end of the island and the water around it. The water was divided into areas of different colors by tide lines and by various depths.

It was clear enough so that we could see the rocks underneath the surface stretching out from the eastern point of the cove. In the cove our tiny skiffs were tied to pinpoint-size buoys. The bright new wood and maroon metal roof of our house glinted through the trees. But the little hill behind the barn hid the corral from our view, so I couldn't see Kenai or the goats. Two miles across the water on the mainland big mountains rose into rugged wilderness. Far across the inlet we could see the Kenai Mountains on the peninsula. The sky was immense. For a long time we sat silently, gazing out over the enormous view, each of us quiet with feelings of insignificance and isolation. In all the land we could see on the west side of the inlet we were the only people. That thought was awesome.

After a while the adult eagles and their young ones flew casually out from behind the west side of the island and across the air below us. "It's nice to know there's another family on the island besides us. Do you think they'll stay around all winter?" I wondered.

"They'll stay if they can find food," Dad responded. "The peregrine falcons will probably stay, too, and the murres will be rafted in open water. There will likely be eider ducks wintering in the cove. And of course the ravens and gray jays and magpies will stay around."

"I did bring a bag of sunflower seeds," Mom chimed in. "I want to put out a feeder and hope we'll have chickadees and redpolls and maybe even some pine grosbeaks, as we did in Anchorage."

"You know, I never realized how interesting and fun birds are until Grandpa Jake started pointing them out to me last year," I said. "This island is full of all kinds of birds in the summertime and I have a goal of being able to recognize all of them on sight. I'd like to learn their songs, too. About the only one I know now is the golden-crowned sparrow. There are a lot of other sparrows and warblers on the island in the summer."

"I'm glad you've learned to enjoy the birds," Mom commented as we stood up and prepared to hike back down the mountain. "I've always loved them."

Monday morning was our first day in our new routine. I came in from feeding the livestock and sat down at my desk. My desk ran across the corner, Mom's was to my right on the other side of the big south window, and Dad's was close to the wood stove on my left. Light streamed in through the windows. I could look out the front window toward the cove and through the south window toward the mountain. My schoolwork was really a correspondence course furnished by the state of Alaska, but since I had no access to mail and couldn't send my work in regularly, Mom and Dad acted as my teachers. I spread out my new books and lesson plans. I was starting out with general mathematics, English composition, basic biology, and United States history. For an elective I chose beginning Spanish since Mom had taken Spanish in high school and college and would be able to help me with it. I was to keep a log of the number of hours I spent riding Kenai, walking briskly, or other body exercise for physical education.

I decided that since math was my weak point, I would do it first thing in the morning and get it over with. Then I'd reward myself with English composition, then do biology, history, and Spanish at the end when it would be least likely to disrupt Mom's writing. It seemed strange to spread out my new notebooks and look into my new books all alone at home without anyone to talk to about them.

Mom typed slowly and irregularly at her typewriter,

staring out the window unseeingly as she composed the next sentence or paragraph or whatever in her head. She had always done her writing while I was at school, and I sort of imagined her sitting there with her fingers flying over the keys as she wrote her stories. Instead she seemed to spend a lot of time thinking and struggling to get the next line down. "Maybe writing books isn't all that different from writing paragraphs for English comp," I thought as I watched her work, "and even though she says she enjoys it, it's hard work."

On my other side, Dad was into some serious reading and notetaking. He intended to write a book called *Trophy Hunting in America*, about his theory that anyone who does well or shows signs of having more ability than most people is likely to get shot down, and how to deal with it. He wanted to incorporate the viewpoints of other writers, so he didn't expect to get started with actual writing for several months. He was collecting examples of his theory that ranged all the way from President Kennedy to gifted high school students.

My math was all review work, and for English comp it was easy to write a paragraph on "How to Harness a Horse." I read the introductions to my biology and U.S. history books and then learned a little about how Spanish pronunciation and spelling work. I decided that Spanish should be a lot easier to pronounce and spell than English because it is more consistent.

We took a fifteen-minute break for tea halfway through the morning but I still finished all my work about an hour before twelve. I went over the second math lesson and polished my paragraph, which Mom would check later in the day.

At noon Mom and I fixed soup and sandwiches for lunch

while Daddy collected the chain saw, the crosscut saw, and everything else we needed for gathering wood. I filled a thermos with tea and packed a waterproof container with pilot bread, peanut butter and honey, and some dried apricots to take along. The weather was cool and crisp, partly cloudy, with a light breeze. We dressed warmly for the boat trip across to the mainland.

After lunch I paddled out in the dinghy to get the yellow boat and bring it to shore. As we left, we swung by the white boat and picked up its single oar so we would have two with us. "In case we get into shallow water and have to pole a long way," Dad said.

Even though it's cold on the water in early September, I love to ride in the boat on those clear, crisp days. The water sparkled and glinted. We headed directly across the channel toward the mainland, then drove south close to the shore looking for a place with a lot of drift logs lying on the beach. Little flocks of shorebirds flew up from their explorations in the gentle surf as we approached. Rafts of scoters swam madly out of the way or waited until the last minute and dived. I sang as I watched the shore for logs and bears, my voice lost in the roar of the motor. I was so completely caught up in the movement of the boat, the water, and the birds that I was startled when the motor coughed. Dad cried, "Oh, no-o-o-!" and the motor sputtered and died. A little plume of smoke floated out from the motor in the total, sudden silence.

"What's wrong?" Mom asked.

"The water pump must have quit and I wasn't paying attention. It looks like I've burned it up."

The lovely sunny day turned chilly. I looked toward the island, a couple of miles away. I could just see Hansons' cabin, very tiny and far off. My heart did a flip.

Mom looked at Daddy. "Can you fix it?"

"It depends how bad it is, but I'm not hopeful," Dad told her soberly. "It's my fault. I should have kept a closer eye on the motor to make sure it was spurting water through the system. It worked so well all summer I just took it for granted. We might as well get in to shore here. I'll see if I can fix it while you two start cutting some wood."

Dad grabbed an oar and handed me the other one. How glad I was that we had picked up that extra oar. The water was shallow enough that we could touch bottom. With the little breeze, as well as the incoming tide pushing us toward land, we quickly poled the boat to the beach. We jumped out and pulled the boat up as far as we could onto the shore. Dad stood in the shallow water at the stern and loosened the bolts that held the motor onto the boat. Grunting, Mom helped him carry the heavy motor onto the beach and lean it against a big log. I carried the little toolbox of emergency tools Dad always kept in the boat.

Mom and I would have liked to stay there hovering over Dad to see what was wrong and if it was fixable, but we weren't any help that way. Besides, there was wood on the beach and it might as well be cut.

"Do you think you can handle the chain saw?" Dad asked Mom. "It's not heavy and it's easy to handle. Just keep a firm grip on it so it doesn't kick back."

That was another thing that amazed me. Before we bought the fishing business, Mom didn't get involved in running things like boat motors and chain saws. She helped carry the wood and stack it when we lived in Anchorage but she left the machinery to Dad. Now she had learned to start and run an outboard motor, she did our laundry in a washing machine powered by a little gas engine, and during the summer she had learned how to run Dad's electric Skil saw and the chain saw. So now we got the chain saw and took it up the beach to a straight bleached gray log about a foot in diameter.

We didn't say anything. It wasn't necessary to tell each other that we were most likely stranded on a lonely beach three miles across water from our island home. The beach we were on sloped gradually up to a low bank. From the bank, forested land climbed steeply up into the forbidding Chignik Mountains. The shoreline itself was cut by numerous rivers and streams and a long inland bay between us and the nearest village at least forty miles to the north. We had to hope that Dad could somehow fix the motor. Our only other chance was to row back to the island with two heavy oars that were meant mainly for pushing the boat off the shore. Using those oars against the tidal currents and the breeze would be. . . . I didn't want to think about it.

Mom started the saw with one firm pull on the rope and it whined and buzzed as she cut into the log. When she had cut through it, I carried the six-foot length to a spot just up the beach from the boat where it would be out of reach of the high tide. Six feet was about the right size for us to handle and haul in the boat. Back at the Snuggery we would cut them into shorter lengths that would fit in the wood stove. These logs had drifted up onto this beach the previous winter and had been drying out all summer long, so the six-foot lengths were just light enough for me to carry unless the log was very thick—then I had to drag it.

Time passed quickly as we worked. Mom had to rest a bit between each cut, but even so she took off first her coat, then her vest, and finally her heavy wool sweater. She worked in her red turtleneck shirt, stopping frequently to wipe the perspiration off her face with her scarf. I shed my layers, too. Hauling wood is hard, heavy work.

But Dad's work was hardest of all. I knew that he felt he *must* make that motor work. He probably spent two hours bent over it with the pieces all pulled apart and spread out on the beach, until he finally stood up. He walked slowly down to where Mom was struggling along with a tough, knotty log. She quit when he got close, shut off the noisy machine, and stood waiting. We could both see that Dad's news was bad. He walked with a huge invisible burden on his back.

"Well," Mom sighed. "What shall we do?"

"I can't fix it. I shouldn't have even bothered to try. There is really only one thing we *can* do and that is, row back. If I'd been thinking, I'd have brought both boats, or brought a spare motor. It's not like in the summer when there are other people around. It didn't even occur to me that today we were truly putting all our eggs in one basket." He sat wearily on the stump of the log Mom was cutting. "We won't try rowing now. We'd be rowing against the tide and the wind, and that would be foolish. We'll do best tomorrow morning when the tide is ebbing and the day breeze isn't blowing yet."

"But Daddy," I burst out, "what about the animals? They won't get fed. Kenai will be terribly . . . ."

"What about us? That snack you brought isn't going to seem like much after we've been cutting wood all afternoon. The animals will be all right. They may dislike not being fed at their regular time but they're fat and healthy. Now let's find a nice sheltered spot where we can build a fire and spend the night. I have a lighter in my pocket and another one in the tool box so we should be able to keep warm and fend off any curious bears. After we've gathered wood for a fire, we'll keep on cutting wood. Annie, you look tired. I shouldn't have let you work alone all this time." Dad gave Mom a tight hug, then he pulled me into the hug, too. He held us so tight I could hardly breathe. Under his breath I heard him say, "Lord, help us."

Mom broke the hugging by saying, "Now, Charlie, you know I'm perfectly capable of cutting this wood. I think I'm in better shape physically than I've ever been in all my life. But my kisses may be a little salty." She laughed and gave Dad a quick kiss.

We soon found a sheltered spot just under the bank where we could build a fire between a couple of huge drift logs. We scavenged up and down the beach until we had gathered an enormous pile of driftwood. Then we each had a few sips of tea from the thermos. "Maybe we can find a freshwater stream close by," Dad said. "After all this hard work we're bound to want more to drink than this thermos of tea."

With Dad handling the chain saw, Mom and I worked the crosscut saw on a couple of big logs. In the next couple hours we had cut a nice amount of wood. During a rest break I located a little freshwater stream about a quarter of a mile away. We all worked together to haul the wood back to the pile I had started.

"I'm glad this is well above the high tide line," Dad remarked, as he surveyed the pile of wood we had stacked. "When we get home we'll bring both boats back and pick this up."

"Just think, no schoolwork tomorrow. But I think I'd rather do schoolwork than row across the channel," I realized.

"It's six o'clock already, imagine that!" Mom exclaimed.

"Let's build our fire and have our meager dinner. If we take the food out of its container we can get some water from that little stream you found up the beach."

"You'd better stay here and guard the food, Mom. Dad and I will go after water."

"Put your sweater and vest back on, Melanie. It's getting cool and you've stopped working so hard. We don't want to get chilled," Mom said, back to her normal self.

We built a roaring fire and Dad and I went up to the stream. It ran down over the bank in a little waterfall so it was easy to catch it in our plastic bucket. We had no way to heat it, not even an old coffee can in the boat, so we would take the risk of drinking it as it was. "We drink the water on the island without boiling it. Why would this be any different?" I asked Dad.

"We don't have any bears on the island," Dad replied. "They can spread parasites and bacteria that could affect humans. But we'll just trust that this will be okay."

Back at our campsite we sat on the ground around the fire, leaning against the big logs. Light from the setting sun shone on the island, our *home* island. I hoped Kenai and the dogs wouldn't be too upset. We ate our pilot bread spread with peanut butter and honey very slowly. Actually I'd packed quite a bit, but we wanted to save some for breakfast. We drank the last of our tea and some of the fresh cold water and ate dried apricots for dessert.

"You know," Dad said, "this is something I really hadn't anticipated. It would be fun camping here if it weren't so serious." I knew that he was concerned that we might just wear out in the middle of the channel tomorrow and end up drifting out into the inlet. Well, we couldn't wear out! Somehow we'd be able to keep up our strength and make it to the island. Still, I couldn't help but remember the time during the summer when one of the people from the tender had tried to row ashore in a dinghy and simply couldn't go anywhere against the tide. He rowed and rowed and just stayed still.

Mom's voice broke into my dire thought. "Well, I thought of such a possibility. You know me. I always think of all the bad things that could happen. But I'm trying to stop doing that and worrying unnecessarily, so I didn't even take my normal precaution of bringing all kinds of extra things along."

"From now on we'll pay attention to your need for extra precaution," Dad announced. "And we won't take any more trips like this without two boats or two motors."

I really didn't think we needed to let this kind of conversation continue. "Let's sing," I suggested.

"That's a good idea," Mom said. We sang all the songs from "The Sound of Music," which I had long ago memorized from listening to the record so much. We sang old hymns and contemporary choruses and gospel songs. Dad piled more wood on the fire, the stars poked holes in the sky, brighter and brighter as the night got darker, a big three-quarter moon rose over the island. We continued to sing. Finally my voice got tired and I faded out. Dad wasn't singing anymore either. Mom's song faded into a soft lullabye:

> Rockabye, hushabye, little papoose,
> The stars come into the sky.
> The whippoorwill's crying, the daylight is dying,
> The river runs murmuring by.
> Dear Manitou loves you,
> And watches above you,
> Till stars of the morning light gleam . . . ."

When I woke up, my body felt stiff and a little achy. I was still sitting up, leaning against the log. The fire was low. Mom lay curled up on her side sleeping on the ground. I looked around. Light filtered across the sky from the east. Dad was down at the boat, which was nearby because it was almost high tide.

With a jerk I realized that we were stranded, getting ready to try to row back across the channel to the island. I shook myself and sat up, fully awake. I got up and put some more wood on the fire. Mom began to stir. She sat up and stretched.

"Did you sleep long?" I asked her. "I must have slept all night. I was so surprised to wake up. I didn't think I'd be able to sleep at all."

"Your dad slept first," she answered. "I sat and watched the stars and moon and listened to the water lapping on shore and the quiet bird calls. I thought we should have someone on watch. Then Charlie woke up when I put some wood on the fire, so I went to sleep. I must have slept three or four hours. What do you think, dear?" she asked Dad as he walked up.

"I think we should get going now while the air is still and it's slack tide. We won't make it before the tide starts to run again, but we'll have much less work."

"Okay, let's quickly have something to eat." Mom stood up and got out the rest of the pilot bread and peanut butter and honey. We each had two crackers, a few fingersful of peanut butter, and some water. We put out our fire, carried the motor down to the boat, and fastened it back on the stern. Dad had already stowed away the saws and toolbox. I put the container of water in the bow.

Dad gave directions. "We will work two at a time, while one person rests. We have no oarlocks or anything to sit on,

51

so one person will stand on each side near the bow and paddle with the oar like you would with a canoe. This boat isn't a rowboat. With proper equipment this trip would be no sweat, but under the circumstances it will be hard work, and we'll get really tired. So we'll rotate. If Melanie and I start out, Anne will take over from Melanie after a while. Then when Melanie has rested a little, she will take my place. I'll rest and then take Anne's place, and so forth. We'll head for a point well to the north of the island, so that when the tide starts to ebb it will carry us toward the island, instead of straight down the channel. Are you ready to go?"

For answer, Mom and I helped push the boat off the beach. Dad and I took the oars and pushed us out until we couldn't touch the bottom anymore. Then we started to paddle. The oars were very long and heavy. I tried to use clean strong strokes—dip, pull, lift; dip, pull, lift; dip, pull, lift.

I was glad for the strength and stamina I had developed from fishing all summer. Riding Kenai had helped, too. I wondered about him. He must be very hungry and upset. Dip, pull, lift; dip, pull, lift—slowly we pulled away from the mainland, but the island didn't look any closer. Mom came and took the oar. "Time for you to rest, Melanie."

I leaned back against the gas can cover in the stern, breathing heavily. Mom and Dad worked in rhythm—dip, pull, lift; dip, pull, lift. It seemed I hadn't rested long before Mom said, "Melanie," and I saw that sweat was pouring down Dad's face. I went up and took his oar. He plopped himself down in the bottom of the boat.

"We're making good progress," Dad said after a while. I looked up. The island did seem closer now. We were about even with the point on the north end. Dip, pull, lift; dip, pull, lift. After a while I realized that Dad had taken Mom's place.

When it was my turn to rest we had slipped a little to the south of the point, the tide had started to run. But we were about halfway across the channel and the tide would soon be pulling us toward a spot on the island where it bent toward the mainland. As long as we reached any place on the island we could walk home at low tide. I knew we would make it now. Knowing that, the work didn't seem quite so hard when I relieved Dad, though I did get tired more quickly. The island got closer and closer. The tide pulled us southward, but we finally reached the shore some distance south of the Hansons' cabin.

"Hooray," I whooped as I jumped out of the boat in water almost to the top of my boots and pulled the bow up to the shore. "Hooray! Hooray! Hooray!" Mom and Dad joined me at the tops of their lungs. "Thank you, God! Thank you, God!"

We used a long rope to tie the boat firmly to a tree up on the bank. We would come back for it at high tide and tow it back with the other boat. We sat and rested on the rocks for a few minutes, but we were too hungry to wait for long, and I was eager to feed my animals. I wondered if they had heard us yelling with joy and were waiting eagerly.

We walked up the beach to where we could cut across the point on the trail. Soon we came out on our own little cove. There was our fishing cabin, all boarded up. And there, oh yes, there was the Snuggery, and behind it the barn and oh, what a welcome—Kenai whinnying, dogs barking impatiently, goats bleating, hens fussing, and even k.c. meowing and brushing against my legs. How glad I was to be home!

Chapter Four

AFTER THAT we did not take a boat away from the island without taking a spare motor or the second boat. We never did have any more trouble with a motor but we weren't going to take the chance.

Slowly we settled into a routine during the month of September. In the mornings we worked at our desks studying and writing. Afternoons we did necessary chores around the house, added to our growing stack of firewood, or cut grass from the point to use for bedding for Kenai and the goats during the winter. We'd stack the cart high with the loose grass and trundle it back to the barn, where we built a real haystack.

All the cottonwood leaves turned gold and dropped off the trees till the ground was covered with a surfeit of gold coins. The devil's club turned scarlet and gold and brown before it succumbed to freezing nighttime temperatures. The leaves on the alders just faded away; by mid-September I noticed the alders were bare.

The young eagles began to soar on the updrafts with their parents. They still had a lot to learn about flying. The summer ducks left and were replaced with eider ducks and old-squaws from far to the north. To them, Cook Inlet was a good place to spend the winter. The gulls and kittiwakes, murres and puffins took off. I wondered where they went. After each storm, fresh snow spread lower on the slopes of the mountains across the channel.

My parents really irritated me sometimes. I guess it was because we all lived so close with no one else around. For some reason when we were working in the mornings, and Mom spent hours contemplating something out the window without touching her typewriter, I felt really annoyed. She expected me to keep working steadily on my school assignments while she simply sat and daydreamed about what she was going to write. When I told her about it she said, "Well, I have to think out what I'm going to say next and how I'm going to say it." I knew that was true, but it still irked me.

Dad bugged me too, always finding so much work to do in the afternoons. He would get going and forget to stop for a break or anything and he expected Mom and me to keep up with him and feel as enthused as he was. Even in the morning when he studied, he was often restless and fidgety. Sometimes I wanted to take time off and take Kenai down to Contemplation Rock in the corner of the cove and just *be*. Dad has a hard time just *being*. He enjoys being active and finds his pleasure in that, but both Mom and I need time for quietness and centering in, or getting things into perspective, as I call it.

Mom finally suggested that we schedule an hour after lunch for everybody to do their own thing, and that helped. When the weather was decent I would ride Kenai around the point or go down to Contemplation Rock, or hike up to Long Jake's cabin, where I could stop and think and let myself become a part of the world around me. If the weather was bad, I went out to the barn to groom Kenai, baked a batch of cookies if Mom wasn't using the kitchen, or sat at the window up in my own bedroom, gazing out the window toward the inlet. Our bedrooms weren't heated except through grating in the floor where the downstairs heat could come up, so I usually had to wrap myself in a blanket.

Mom used those times to take walks and hikes, too. Occasionally we'd go together. But Dad nearly always worked on one of his many projects or cut the wood into stove lengths and split it. Often we'd come back after an hour and find him already started with whatever our work was for that day. That's how he got things into perspective for himself.

Having that hour each day helped a little with my irritation, but I still was frustrated with them at times. For some reason I was fed up with hugging and usually pushed Mom or Dad away if they tried to hug me or even just pat me on the shoulder. I didn't want to be touched. I don't know why, but that fall, touching really irked me.

Toward the end of September, when the sky was overcast and gray every day and we could feel snow in the air, and I had to knock a coating of ice off the livestock water every morning, I decided I wanted to spend a weekend all by myself up in Long Jake's cabin. We had plenty of firewood ahead, so we didn't need to spend Saturday going after wood, and we had cut all the hay we needed. Those projects were ones we had wanted to do before it snowed; now we were ready for snow, so I could take the time off.

On Friday evening I loaded Kenai with my warm sleeping bag, food for him and Talkeetna and me, and a couple of books. Dad had gone up with me the day before to make sure the stovepipe was clean and there was enough wood split. Mom insisted on that. She didn't want me to have a cabin fire or to cut myself splitting wood while I was all alone.

I reassured her, "Mom, I'll be fine. I won't do anything dangerous. I'm just going to read and relax and do some hiking. I'll keep Talkie with me all the time so if anything bad happens, which it won't, she can come after you. She will, you know."

"Well," Mom repeated for the twentieth time, "be careful. You can come back down if you get lonely."

"I know, Mom. I don't want you coming up there to check on me either. I'm old enough to take care of myself, and I want to be alone. I'll be fine."

"Of course you will," Dad laughed. "Now get going. Mom and I are going to have a good time together while you're gone. Maybe we'll even go out to dinner!"

"Now, Charlie," Mom protested with a smile. I didn't hear how Dad was going to take her out to dinner because I was already headed up the trail, leading Kenai with Talkeetna gamboling around us. Goofus cried about being left behind, but he soon stopped and I guessed that Mom and Dad had taken him along into the house with them.

The trail to Long Jake's cabin was a lot different from when I had first gone up to see him, more than a year ago. The clearing where the wild irises had bloomed all blue and purple was grown over with tall brown grasses, tangled and broken by the rain and wind. The alders were bare, short, stubby trees all twisted around each other. The spiny devil's club that had covered the ground in nasty but attractive bushes was now just piles of broad leaves rotting on the ground. The glorious golden leaves and crisp bright air of autumn were gone. The whole island seemed to be waiting for the first blanket of soft, white snow.

It was still hard for me to climb the hill without expecting to see Long Jake waiting for me in the clearing and the sharp pain of realizing he was gone. But the good feeling of anticipation, of looking forward to new things, was there. Walking over the last ridge and into the clearing was a little like coming home.

I put Kenai in the little goat pen. Dad and I had enlarged the door so that he could go into the tiny barn for shelter. Talkeetna went into the cabin with me. I had packed Long Jake's few clothes away; otherwise the cabin was the same as always. The long low bed in the back with shelves over it for clothes and other personal things, the bookshelves along one side with all of Long Jake's books, were still there. Many of them were ornithology books, filled with fascinating details about birds. I had identified a number of birds during the summer and had learned something about their habits and what their lives were like from these books.

Under the southeast-facing window stood the table with shelves for dishes and pans and food spanning the corner between the window and the door. On the other side of the door was the stove, which served as cookstove and heater. Long Jake had long ago painted the walls and peaked ceiling white, giving the cabin a fairly light feeling. The only color in the room came from the book covers and the striped Hudson Bay blanket on the bed. I decided I would bring a couple of posters to hang on the walls and make some bright curtains for the window to make the cabin cheerier.

I put my food away and stashed my sleeping bag in a corner of the bed. With my sharp pocketknife I carefully made some shavings from a piece of split wood and started a fire in the stove. Then I took a bucket and went up the path to the spring. Long Jake had built a wooden reservoir for the water and a lean-to over it to keep out dirt and snow. I dipped my bucket into the pool of water and carried it back to the barn, where I poured it into the galvanized tub for Kenai. It took several trips to the spring before I had enough water for Kenai; the last bucketful was for me.

Back in the cabin the fire crackled cheerfully. I put some water on to boil for macaroni, then cut some Velveeta cheese to have with it and sliced some Spam very thin to fry. Most of our food for the winter had to be dried or canned, though we had a supply of potatoes and carrots and some cabbages. And now that the weather was getting colder, Dad hoped soon to shoot a moose on the mainland so we could have canned and frozen moose meat. He'd been watching for moose on our forays to the mainland for wood and knew where to find a young bull. But he wanted to wait until the last days of moose season so that it would be cold and the meat wouldn't spoil.

I opened a can of peas and put half of them on the stove to heat. Soon I had a fine dinner ready. I gave Talkie her food so she wouldn't have to beg for mine and sat down at the little table to eat. I felt very peaceful sitting there eating my meal.

I was alone but not lonely. I could see Kenai standing quietly inside the fence. The gray sky grew grayer with dusk. I ate some dried apples and oatmeal cookies for dessert, then I lighted the kerosene lamp and set it on the table while I washed up my pans and dishes. It was almost dark when I went out to feed Kenai. When I feed Kenai I don't get to talk to him much or pet his nose. He is interested only in eating. So I left him and went back into the warm cabin.

I put more wood in the stove and opened the book I had brought along to start reading, *Jane Eyre*. When I read, I become so involved with the characters and the story I forget all about the time and place. Before long I was far away in 19th-century England, far, far away from a little cabin in Alaska in the 1980s.

Finally I began to feel chilly and realized that I'd let my fire burn way down. It was almost out. I stirred up the coals and put on more wood, then made a trip out to the "biffy" and got ready for bed. I filled up the stove and turned down the draft, hoping the fire would last most of the night at least. Then I blew out the lamp and crawled into the bed. Talkie curled up on the floor beside me.

I woke up suddenly. When I opened my eyes the light was gray and flickering and my nose was cold. I hopped out of bed and looked out the window. Snow! Several inches already covered the ground, piled up on the fence posts and railings, and lay in soft pillows along the alder branches. Large, fluffy flakes continued to fall thickly. The whole world was transformed in one night from the bare, sodden bleakness of late fall into the white and purple fairyland of snow. I shivered and pulled on my clothes that I'd hung over the back of a chair near the stove. The stove still felt a little warm but the fire was out. Quickly I built a new fire and put water on for tea. I let Talkie out and she went romping through the snow, delighted. She shoved her nose into it and tossed it. Her mouth hung open in a silly grin. In a moment I pulled on my coat and boots and went out to run with her.

The snow was wet enough to make snowballs. I formed a little snowball and threw it. Talkie went after it, but when she picked it up it disintegrated in her mouth. I kept throwing snowballs and she kept trying to pick them up and bring them back to me, shaking her head in puzzlement. I laughed until I could hardly throw snowballs anymore. The flakes fell so fast I soon blended in with the scenery.

Kenai came out of the barn to see what was happening. He nickered with pleasure when I kissed him on his snowy nose. Soon he was covered with snow, too. It felt glorious to celebrate the first snow of winter all alone with Talkeetna and Kenai. Finally I fed Kenai his breakfast and got the bucket. I made my way through the fairyland to the spring, careful not to bump the tree branches that hung overhead so I wouldn't get a neckful of snow.

Back in the cabin I fixed myself a soft-boiled egg and toast and ate a half can of grapefruit sections. Then I went back outdoors and got Kenai ready to hike on up the mountain with me. I had planned to ride him but I was afraid the trail might be a little slippery with the fresh snow, so I led him instead. We started up the trail in the falling snow. Our tracks were the only thing to change the pure smooth cover of white, but the snow seemed determined to wipe them out too.

We climbed way up above the tree line, where we could have seen far out over the inlet if it hadn't been snowing. Now all we could see was a curtain of falling snow. Kenai snorted and then stood still. Talkie, who had romped and explored all the way up, now sat down beside me, her ears pointed forward alertly. The snow fell with a silence so complete you could hear it, a perfect muffled quietness. I tried to hold my breath so it would not interrupt the silence, but Kenai didn't hold his. He breathed in little puffs of steam. His breathing sounded loud in that wide, wild hush of snow.

We stayed so long on the mountain that the snow began to pile up on us in soft cushions and the tracks we had made completely disappeared. But we knew where the trail was. Talkeetna scurried ahead, sniffing and snuffling in the snow. She buried her nose in it and came out looking whiter than ever, with snowy eyelashes and a little pile of snow on her nose. I had to keep laughing at her, but she laughed with me. Kenai plodded along. He snorted at the snow on his nose and shied whenever a little pile of snow fell, plop, off a branch right in our path. We walked joyfully down the mountain.

After I had brushed Kenai off and given him water, and then swept the snow off myself, I built up the fire again. Then I fixed myself a Spam sandwich and a cup of hot mint tea.

It was a perfect afternoon to curl up in the cabin with a crackling fire and read. I need to do that sort of thing once in a while. I buried myself in *Jane Eyre*. Every once in a while I stretched and added wood to the fire and fixed myself a cup of hot chocolate. When it got too dark to read, I realized that it was dinnertime. I hurried out to feed Kenai. Inside, I lit the lamp and heated a can of hearty beef-vegetable soup. I thought, "Everyone my age ought to have a chance to be alone like this once in a while, to fix their own food and take care of themselves for a couple of days."

I felt very capable and strong. I was completely responsible for myself and for Kenai and Talkeetna. I had to observe basic rules of safety in the cabin and the woods, but I could do whatever I wanted to within those limitations. It was strange how important it seemed to observe a schedule for eating and feeding the animals and sleeping. That helped to define the day, but it also made me feel free to do what I wanted to with the rest of my time. If I had read as long as I wanted to without stopping and just eaten whenever I felt hungry enough and fed the animals when they begged for it, I think I would have felt lonely and chaotic, sort of like floundering around in the water without being able to touch bottom. Structuring the day helped me to feel like I had a base. But I don't know exactly why.

After dinner I played a few games of solitaire and popped a bowlful of popcorn. I put *Jane Eyre* aside and looked through Long Jake's books. The study of murres caught my eye. Murres are such neat little birds, with their black backs and heads and snowy breasts. They look like little penguins standing upright on the little rock shelves where they lay their eggs. They float on the water in huge groups or rafts and if they are startled they must really struggle to get airborne because their feet are so far back and their wings are so small for the rest of their bodies. Their wings beat madly when they fly. They can't glide, so when they want to land on a tiny ledge on a cliff they must suddenly put on the brakes and plop down. I've seen them miss and go around again. Sometimes one must make several passes before she lands appropriately in the right spot.

Since murres don't build much of a nest and they lay their eggs on narrow ledges of rock on the steep sides of cliffs, their eggs are pointed at one end. When they roll they simply go in a circle around that point instead of rolling off the ledge. The babies hatch late in the summer and don't learn to fly before fall. When the parents are ready to move out into open water, where they spend the winter in huge rafts, they swim around under the cliff and call to the babies to come. The little ones finally jump out of the nests and fall into the sea, where an adult, usually the father, cares for them and teaches them how to dive and catch the little sand lances that are their main diet.

Sand lances are tiny fish that have the ability to burrow into the sand and stay there when the tide goes out, until it rises again. The murres dive to catch them—they don't dig them out of the sand. When the sand lances are scarce for some reason, the murres don't nest that year. Long Jake had studied them over many years and watched their population fluctuate up and down, depending on the weather and food conditions.

It's risky to be a murre chick. One can get swept off the cliff in a storm or carried off and eaten by eagles or falcons or glaucous gulls. If it survives all that it must finally make that perilous tumble into the sea from high up on a cliff and, of course, many of the chicks end up crashing on the rocks below.

Long Jake had banded a number of common murres and studied as many of those specific birds as he could follow over a period of years. I was fascinated by his story of their lives. He became very attached to them and had names for each one.

The snowfall was thinning out when I went to bed that night and in the morning the sun was shining. Oh, what a world! A million diamonds sparkled and twinkled in the dazzle. The sky was deep deep blue. The air snapped and crackled. The snow squeaked under my feet as I carried water from the spring. But it was still early fall, and by noon, when I had finished reading *Jane Eyre*, everything was dripping. Big chunks of snow fell off the cabin and barn roofs and out of the alders. Water dripped off the eaves. I made my lunch of leftovers from the previous meals and cleaned the cabin carefully. I wanted to make sure there were no crumbs or anything to attract mice and weasels. I let the fire die and made sure it was out before I packed my sleeping bag and books and closed the cabin. I loaded everything on Kenai and led him down the hill. We had to go slowly because the wet, melting snow was slippery and Kenai had to make sure of his footing with each step.

It had been a lovely weekend for me and I felt refreshed and better able to tolerate my parents again. They actually acted glad to see me. Apparently they missed me a little bit.

The temperatures were dipping below freezing each night and the moose season was nearly over, so Dad decided we should take off a couple of days to go moose hunting. We hadn't wanted to count on getting a moose in case we didn't, so we had enough other protein to last the winter. But frozen moose steaks and liver and roasts would certainly improve the quality of our meals.

We packed our tent and sleeping bags and enough food for a couple of days for Dad and me. Mom had decided to be the one to stay home and look after the animals. Since I love animals so much I wasn't at all sure I wanted to go along on a moose hunt, but I also like eating meat—I guess that's an inconsistent thing about me—so I figured I'd have to think of the moose as meat. Dad would be doing the actual hunting and shooting anyway. I would stay at camp and be available to help cut it up and pack the meat out to the boat. I did have a rifle to keep with me; Dad taught me how to use it in case of bears. But it was cold enough that bears weren't likely to bother us.

We took one boat with an extra motor. That way, Mom would have the other boat available if she needed it. We left Tuesday afternoon, following many admonitions from Mom, who insisted that we follow all her warnings so she wouldn't have to worry. It seemed to me that she would find something to worry about anyway, so why bother? But I guess it's always harder to be the one left behind. I had to give her strict instructions about taking care of Kenai since she was still not at all comfortable around him.

We drove our boat across to the mainland and into a little cove. While we were getting wood, Dad had discovered a meadow with plenty of signs of moose in the marshy flat ground around the cove. Then to his delight he had even seen a small bull that would be just right for our winter's supply of meat. He wanted to set up camp on the beach and hike to the meadow just before dusk, when the moose come out to feed. It was only about five hundred yards or so to the meadow but the ground was marshy, with patches of snow still left in shady spots and many windfalls and thickets of alders. So Dad was grateful for clear skies and a moon to light his way back out after dark. Unless he was lucky that first evening he intended to go back in again at dawn.

A chilly breeze blew off the water while we set up our little tent in the shelter of a large tree root. I built a nice camp fire while Dad heated on the tiny camp stove the baked beans Mom had made for us. We ate an early dinner of beans and crisp cabbage leaves and bread, with a can of apricots for dessert. We were bundled up pretty warmly already, but Dad put on his down winter coat, took his gun, and headed down the beach to where he planned to hike in to the meadow. "Keep the fire going," he admonished me before he left. "It will help me to find you when I'm coming back, and I'll probably be cold."

I read for a while after he left. I didn't hear any gunshots. It was probably two hours later when I realized that I was really struggling to see the words in my book. It was dark; the fire was low. I got a roaring fire going again, but it really didn't provide enough light to read by. So I put my sleeping bag down on a foam pad near the fire, leaned back against a log, and gazed at the stars. Up there was a big dipper and the north star, the symbols on Alaska's simple state flag, of which we all felt very proud. Tonight I imagined the big dipper as a moose stalking across the sky. And there was Orion, hunting it. Over the ages Orion had never caught that sky moose. I hoped Dad would have better luck.

In a path across the heavens the stars of the milky way clustered like a cloud. I could not begin to comprehend how vast a space they covered, nor how far away they were. I lay there for a long time trying to imagine. The moon rose, about a three-quarter moon, and climbed quite a distance up into the sky before I realized that Dad should have long since arrived at the camp. He could not hunt after dark; he should have headed back as soon as it got too dark to hunt. Without a watch I couldn't tell what time it was, but I knew that it was very late.

I stood up, feeling a bit stiff, and put more wood on the fire. I didn't know for sure what to do. I knew Dad didn't want to disturb the moose and make them wary by shooting off a gun except in an emergency, but I didn't know if this was an emergency. Dad hadn't really said anything about *when* he'd be back.

Suddenly I felt panic flooding over me like a wave. My heart began to beat wildly. My chest felt like it was being squeezed in a vice, and I could hardly breathe. My hands and knees trembled. Frightening thoughts that really didn't make any sense raced through my brain. I felt tears starting just behind my eyes. A sob caught in my throat. "Oh Dad, my dear, beloved Daddy, where are you? Daddy, you *must* be okay. What happened?"

Even as I panicked, I knew that I must not. I needed to maintain a cool head and be strong. With great effort I took a deep breath and firmly took myself into control. "Now calm down, take deep breaths, sit down on the log, and *think*." Slowly I got my body back into line so I could concentrate on the possibilities. "If Daddy were hurt, he would have fired three shots in quick succession to let me know. If he were hopelessly lost he would do that too. What else could happen? Nothing. Either he is somewhat lost and has decided to wait till daylight because it would be too dark for me to find him now anyway, or he has decided to stay right at the meadow until morning. He dressed very warmly, and he took a canteen of water and some granola bars. He would definitely not want me to go into the woods in the middle of the night to look for him. I need to stay here and keep the fire going and wait until morning to decide what to do."

That was a long night. I fed the fire and fought panic. I took my sleeping bag out of the tent and put it on my sleeping mat by the fire and climbed in but I couldn't sleep. Mom wasn't there to sing lullabies. I was all alone with no one to take care of me. In fact, we were all three alone in separate places. I actually hoped Mom was worrying because then I knew she would pray extra hard for us, and Daddy and I both needed all the prayers we could get.

I prayed myself, but it was hard to do. Somehow I couldn't put my fears into words; doing that might make them true. So I just reached out to God and it seemed almost like he was putting his hand down through the milky way to me. The moon climbed high among the stars and began to drop down toward the mountain.

Finally I could see the shape of Gresham Island against the sky to the east. Dawn was coming! Slowly the eastern sky lightened. I stood up and stretched and walked down to the edge of the water. The yellow boat rocked lightly from side to side, up and down in the choppy waves. I felt hungry. There was no reason not to eat. In fact, eating would help me think more clearly when I had to decide what to do. I put a pot of water on the fire to heat and began to slice boiled potatoes into the frying pan.

Suddenly a loud crash broke into the stillness of the morning. It came from the woods and echoed from the hills on the other side of the cove. A gunshot! I stood up and listened for two more to follow in quick succession, but the air stopped vibrating and again there was only the sound of the water slapping the shore, the crackling of the fire, the sizzling of the potatoes in the pan.

"Dad must have shot a moose! Oh, joy! He is okay! Oh, wonderful!" I began to dance around, jumping up and down with happiness. I didn't care whether he'd hit the moose or not, so long as Daddy was okay.

As I calmed down enough to add a couple of eggs to my potatoes another gunshot rocked the air around the cove. "Well, either he missed the first time or that was the kill shot," I thought. Kent had told me about a man who thought his moose was dead and went up to it, to begin gutting it, when the moose suddenly stood up and ran off into the woods. The hunter was so startled he let it go.

Kent's advice was to make sure the moose was dead by shooting it in the head before starting to gut it. So now I hoped that Dad had just made that kill shot. If he had shot a moose, he wouldn't come back until he had gutted and maybe skinned it. He had promised me that I would not have to see it until it looked more like meat than a moose.

Breakfast tasted delicious! Knowing Dad must be okay made all the difference. Even though I hadn't slept I felt good and happy. I built up the fire, set the pot of water close to keep hot, and settled down with a cup of hot chocolate and my book to wait for Dad.

Hours later he came dragging up the beach. With a shout of joy I ran to meet him and flung my arms around him, bloody trousers, heavy backpack, gun and all. He looked very tired but he was grinning as he hugged me back.

"I hope you have something hot for me to drink," he smiled as I practically led him back to the camp. "I'm bushed. It's not easy to sleep sitting up against a tree all night."

"Oh, Daddy, what happened? Why didn't you come back last night?" I tried not to show how worried I had been.

"Well, when I got to the meadow I saw a moose and I couldn't believe my luck, but when I got closer I saw that it was a cow. Then I saw another cow at the edge of the meadow near the trees. I figured that at this time of year if there are cows around there's bound to be a bull or two, so I waited, hoping one would show up. The cows didn't seem to know I was there. They ate quietly and then moved off into the woods. I was just about ready to give up and come back when I heard some snorting and crashing around off to the right. By then the light was getting bad and I could barely see. But sure enough the moose came to the edge of the woods and I could just make out the rack. There was my bull! But it was too dark and I was too far away to get a good shot. The bull messed around for a while on that side of the meadow, and then—what do you know?–he bedded down for the night right there at the edge of the trees! All I had to do was get close enough for a good shot and wait until morning. So that's what I did. I got a little cold in the night, but not too bad. I didn't want to move around too much and scare that moose away, but he stayed put. This morning when he got up I could easily see him and now we have our meat!"

While he talked Dad opened his backpack and pulled out pieces of meat: the heart and liver and tongue. He sliced a couple of thin pieces of liver and put them in the frying pan. I cut up more potatoes and an onion to fry with it. What a feast! Fresh moose liver is delicious. You fry it only enough to brown it and it melts in your mouth. A lot of my friends at school don't like liver but they have never tasted fresh moose liver cooked over an open fire in hunting camp.

Now that I knew Dad was safe I felt a little angry with him for not letting me know he might be gone all night. "Daddy, why didn't you tell me you might not come back last night? I didn't sleep at all. I didn't know what might have happened to you."

"But I warned you of that possibility, Melanie. I thought you knew."

This is one of Dad's weaknesses. He knows something in his own mind and he thinks to himself that he must tell Mom and me and then somehow, before he gets around to telling us he assumes we know it. It is very frustrating for him and for us. He thinks we are very forgetful, and he always argues that he has told us, but it has happened so often that Mom and I know better. Even his secretary back in Anchorage said he did that with her. Now I explained carefully, "Daddy, you told me that you were going into the woods until it was too dark to hunt. You said that if you needed me you would fire three shots in quick succession, several minutes apart so I could find you, and that otherwise I was to stay right here. But you didn't tell me that you might *choose* to stay in the woods all night."

"Well, I'm sorry, Melanie. I was sure I told you I might stay." Dad looked a little sheepish.

"Anyway, you are back safe and sound now and I forgive you," I said. "But I think it was the worst night of my life. I just kept telling myself that you must be okay or you would signal me. Please try not to do that to me again, Daddy."

"I'll do my best, Mel. Now, get your packboard. We have a long afternoon of packing meat ahead of us. I don't want to leave the meat there for long in case there are any bears around."

We cut ourselves a better trail as we hiked back to the meadow. It really wasn't very far. With his meat saw and knife, Dad cut the moose into pieces that we could handle. Even then they were heavy. Dad tied a piece of meat unto my packboard and helped me get it on. Then I helped him load a piece at least twice as big on his back and we headed slowly for the beach, almost staggering. At the beach we dumped our loads on a piece of heavy plastic, pulled the boat into shore, and loaded our meat into it, covering it carefully to keep the gulls off. Then after a short rest we trudged wearily back to the meadow. I don't know how many trips we made that afternoon, but by dusk we had all the meat packed out. The sky was gray and overcast and

72

the air was turning colder. My body felt like it had been run over by a road grader.

"I think we would be better off waiting until high tide tomorrow morning to cross back to the island," Dad said. "I don't believe it will get rough. Let's build a fire and cook a couple of steaks and then we can hit the sack."

I could hardly stay upright to eat my steak and potatoes and fresh cabbage leaves, but it was welcome after all the hard work. I cleaned up the dishes while Dad went to check that the boat was securely anchored, then I climbed into my sleeping bag and didn't wake up until morning.

Before noon we motored into the cove. Mom hurried down to the beach to meet us. It's a wonder she could figure out what had happened as Dad and I kept interrupting each other to tell her the story. By evening the meat we wanted to freeze was stored carefully in a little meat cache Dad had built up on stilts so the weasels and martens couldn't get into it. He wrapped the stilts with tin to keep the animals from climbing up. We climbed a ladder to get to the meat, but had to put the ladder down each time we finished using it. The rest of the meat we canned in quart jars over the next several afternoons. Meanwhile we slipped back into the routine of studying and writing in the mornings.

Chapter Five

SNOW FELL AGAIN in early October and this time it didn't melt away. Every morning I had to break ice off the water barrel in the barn before I could water the animals. The trip down to the waterfall to get water was treacherous, with slippery rocks. We still took Kenai and the cart but I had to lead him slowly and carefully so he wouldn't slip. Ice was building up around the base of the falls, and each time we went for water the icicles on the rocks beside the falls were longer and thicker. The waterfall began to dwindle as it froze, so it took longer and longer to fill our water buckets and jugs. We used water sparingly, taking showers only once a week. We never poured any good water down the drain.

Dad kept hoping for more snow and it did accumulate slowly, but we still didn't have much snow to melt when the waterfall froze completely. We had to break a trail through the snow up to Jake's spring, which normally stays open all winter because the water comes up out of the ground at a temperature a little above freezing. That was a long way to go to get water, leading Kenai carefully along the slippery trail. Actually Kenai himself drank as much water or more than we used in the house, so I began to gather as much snow as possible to melt in the barn water barrel.

Kenai and the goats grew long shaggy winter coats. I teased Kenai that he looked like a huge teddy bear. The dogs' fur got thick. The chickens stayed indoors all the time and fluffed out their feathers to keep warm. When we started melting snow in the water barrel, we kept the kerosene heater burning. The chickens usually huddled together on a shelf against the heated wall.

Early in November we had a snowstorm that lasted three days. Snow piled high everywhere. Each morning Dad and I had to shovel a new path to the barn, and the banks on either side of it got higher and higher. Usually when it snows in Alaska there is no wind and the snow just piles up silently, but this storm came with wind howling around the house and waves crashing against the beach. We were reminded of the blizzards in the Laura Ingalls Wilder Little House books. "Let the hurricane roar!" Dad quoted Laura's pa. "We are snug in our cozy house and barn and we have plenty of food for the whole winter! Now we'll have plenty of snow to melt for water, too. I'm glad it's windy because that will pack the snow into drifts and we can cut blocks of it instead of having to pack it into buckets."

When I awoke on the fourth morning the wind was calm and the waves had subsided into long swells breaking on the beach in a soothing rhythm. The air in my bedroom felt like ice in my nose. I pulled my clothes under the covers and kept them there to warm up a bit before putting them on, still in bed. I gathered all my courage and flung the covers off. Br-r-r, it was cold! Quickly, I made the bed and glanced out the window. The sky was clear, but the sun still hid behind the cliff on the other side of the cove. As far as I could see the island was soft and white except on the beach where the water kept the snow washed off the rocks and gravel. A bunch of old squaws and eider ducks swam lazily in the cove. My teeth began to chatter. I hurried downstairs. Dad was putting wood into the heating stove in the living room, which he now stoked to burn all night. So the living area and the kitchen were warm from the stoves, but not much leaked upstairs through the grates in the ceiling.

"What's for breakfast?" I asked Mom as I put some hot water from the teakettle into the basin to wash my face.

"I'm going to fry some cornmeal mush and a couple of little moose steaks. When you're washed up, will you set the table and pour juice? I think we need to mix some milk, too." Mom put a few drops of vegetable oil right on the smooth top of the oil stove, which made an excellent griddle, and spread it around with a spatula. I put three yellow quilted place mats on the table and set our places. Mom kept an African violet with several deep purple blooms in the middle of the table. She thinks mealtime is much more pleasant if the table looks pretty. In Anchorage she often buys one or two stems of daisies to make a cheerful centerpiece during the dark winter months, and we nearly always have a candle burning on the table during dinner. I poured the juice, filled the pitcher with water from the water barrel, which was getting low, and measured the powdered milk into it, stirring it vigorously to make sure no lumps remained. I've drunk powdered milk for almost as long as I can remember and I'm so used to it that fresh whole milk tastes too rich for me. I think of goat milk as another drink entirely.

Before breakfast was ready Dad stuck his head out the porch door to see the thermometer. "It's hanging right around zero," he announced, hurrying back into the house. "This is our first cold spell."

We sat down to breakfast. Mom read Psalm 30. The part that I liked was "Tears may linger at nightfall, but joy comes in the morning." After we thanked God for our breakfast, I said, "Even the weather confirms that verse, 'joy comes in the morning.' Last night it was still stormy and I was feeling depressed and irritable. I was really getting tired of being stuck in the house with you two. Now the sun is shining and I feel much better. I could sing, even." I spread apple butter on my fried mush and settled down to eat.

"You're right," Mom remarked. "It seems like if we wait long enough and don't give up hope, joy usually does come sometime after sorrow, and the sun shines after a storm. But we probably wouldn't really appreciate the sunshine if we didn't have the storms, and I don't think we could really feel joy if we didn't feel sorrow and pain and anger as well."

"By definition, you can't have one without the other, I suspect," Dad said. "Could you know you were feeling joyful if you have never felt sorrow or pain? Isn't joy the absence of sorrow and vice versa?"

"Not necessarily," Mom replied. "I think joy can be a kind of peace and contentment and victory that a person can feel even in the midst of deep pain or sorrow. It's a sense of being loved and cared for even in suffering. Remember last spring, Melanie, when you finally accepted Jake's death? It was agony for you. But you sang with real joy in your voice on your way down the hill after the memorial service. Weren't you still feeling pain?"

"Oh, yes, I was. I still do, often. But I feel sure that in spite of my loneliness for Grandpa Jake somehow everything is going to be all right. There for a while it seemed like it couldn't, but when I thought I couldn't bear it you both cared about how I felt and helped me carry my pain. I know you love me and God loves me."

"You have hope, in other words," Dad said. "Maybe joy has something to do with hope. As long as one has hope, a person can't be completely destroyed." He paused, thinking. "Well, that's faith, too. Confidence that everything is going to be all right, that God will not fail, and acting on the smallest shred of that confidence, is faith. You were acting on faith that night we were moose hunting when you were scared to death about me but didn't go running willy-nilly into the woods to look for me."

"Well, I didn't have all that much faith, Dad. I had to fight panic all night. But joy came in the morning!" I laughed.

"You're right about that. You should have seen your face." Dad's eyes crinkled up in a warm smile. "Well, Mel, we have to shovel the path again this morning. The animals will be waiting. Maybe this path will keep for a while."

We put on warm clothes and boots and stepped outdoors into a dazzling morning, so bright and cold it took my breath away. The snow glittered and squeaked under our footsteps. "It's good we built a shelter for the woodpile. Look at that," Dad remarked as we grabbed our shovels.

The top of the shelter was level with the snowdrift behind it. The piles of snow we had already thrown up on either side of the path made it look more like a tunnel. We set to work shoveling snow and throwing it up to the tops of those walls. Deep snow mounded the roof of the barn and lay half way up its sides.

"The barn should stay nice and warm with so much snow around it," Dad said. "It will help insulate the house, too."

As we got close to the barn I said, "I need to clean out the stalls and put fresh bedding down this afternoon. I haven't done it since the storm began. I'll have to clear the snow away from the door into the corral and uncover the haystack. I guess I have my afternoon's work cut out for me."

"Since you have to do that, I guess Anne and I can cut snow blocks for water," Dad said. "That will be a daily chore from now on because when the snow melts the volume decreases considerably. We'll have to fill the water barrels with snow each day and by the next day it will be melted down enough so we can add more. I want to take it from the drift along the top of the bank all along the beach, so be careful not to walk there or let the animals walk there."

Kenai snorted and nosed into my coat pockets to see if I had a treat for him, and the goats crowded up to the wall of the stall on the other side. I fed them all and put water into their tubs. Dad found a couple of eggs in the hens' nests. The chickens were huddled together against the wall that was warm from the kerosene heater beside the water barrel, but they seemed none the worse for the cold. They were glad to be fed.

By the time we got back into the house Mom had

finished the breakfast dishes. She filled the kettle with water and set it on the cook stove to heat while Dad and I rubbed our cold hands together over the wood stove, stamped our feet, and blew cold air out of our lungs so we could breathe in the warm air. Then we sat down to work. The sun shone brightly through the windows. The house felt cozy and warm. I tackled my math. Mom typed erratically between sessions of deep thinking. Dad organized note cards full of his tiny illegible handwriting. I don't see how he reads it himself, much less expects other people to read it, but Mom says she learned to read Dad's writing when he wrote letters to her before they were married and she doesn't think it's all that bad.

The forenoon went by quickly, with one coffee break at ten o'clock. I had hot tea with one of Mom's homemade English muffins, toasted, with butter and wild blueberry jam. For the last half hour, Mom quit writing and helped me with my Spanish. She said she was glad for the diversion, because writing wore her out. "I enjoy it," she said, "but it's a struggle, and sometimes it's emotionally exhausting too. I get so involved with the characters I almost live their lives. I go to sleep at night thinking about what is going to happen to them the next day."

At noon we all left our desks. Dad fixed the wood fire while Mom and I made lunch. I peeled potatoes and cut them up into little cubes. Mom put them in a pan, covered them with water, and put them on to boil. She chopped a bit of onion to put in and we added some dried celery leaves since we didn't have celery to flavor it with. When the potatoes were soft we added a can of evaporated milk and a sliced hard-boiled egg. Delicious potato soup for lunch! We had pilot bread crackers with peanut butter and honey, and canned peaches as well.

After lunch was our hour of private time. I bundled up again and went out into the bright cold day. I let Goofus and Talkeetna loose. They went loco running around in the snow like crazy. They dashed around, dug their noses into the snow, and played with each other. I cleared the snow away from the outside of the corral door and the corral gate so I could open them, then led Kenai out. He got all excited, too. How the world had changed in three days while he was penned up inside the barn! He stepped rather gingerly in the snow and shied at everything. I led him down to the beach. It was half-tide so there was plenty of bare beach to walk on, but we had to be careful of the rocks and gravel which were covered with ice. Ice was even forming on the top of the water like a thin flexible skin.

Kenai's breath made clouds of steam; mine caught in the folds of the scarf I had wrapped around my face and made it icy. We walked down to Contemplation Rock and back. Kenai huffed and puffed steam and snorted and danced the whole way. He wanted to run, but of course it was too icy. The dogs ran in circles around us. It was so cold the trees creaked and cracked, the waves tinkled with breaking ice as they washed against the shore, the rhythm of Dad's ax, splitting wood, rang clearly in the cold air. The dogs grinned with joy.

Back at the barn I let Kenai and the goats out into the corral while I mucked out their stalls and cleaned the chicken pen. I carried it all to the corral door and loaded it into the big cart, which was difficult to maneuver in the snow. I had to call Dad from cutting snow blocks with a great big machete-like knife to help me push the cart out of the corral and dump it. Dad planned to use the old bedding as mulch on our garden in the spring. The haystack was covered with heavy plastic. I climbed up and pushed off all the snow, then uncovered one corner and forked the hay into the cart. Dad came again to help me take the cart back into the corral and I spread clean hay on the floors of each stall. What a job! I felt exhausted.

Meanwhile, Dad and Mom took the small cart, which was kept clean specifically for this purpose, and filled it with snow blocks, each about eighteen inches square. First they filled the water barrel in the barn with several blocks which would slowly melt in the water already there. Then they filled the barrel in the house. That would melt more quickly because it was warmer in the house.

It was almost four o'clock and the sun was dropping close to the mountains on the mainland when I finished my job. Mom had a cup of hot chocolate ready for me. I sat and rested for a while. Dad, who always wished for time to do some woodworking, was sanding some pieces of wood in the entry hallway, where it would make the least mess. He was building a proper plant stand for Mom. Mom had already put a moose roast on to cook, and was quilting a patchwork pillow top. After I had rested, I got out the drift-wood mobile I was making for Grandpa and Grandma for Christmas. We were hoping they would be able to charter a helicopter and come to the island for a week at Christmas. So we were making gifts for them and for Uncle Kent and Uncle Greg and his new wife, Karen, and for Aunt Rose. We also made gifts for Dad's family to send along out with them. Before long it got too dark to work and I lit the lamps and hung them from hooks on the ceiling in the living room, work area, and kitchen. Then I dressed in boots, coat, scarf, and gloves and hurried out to the barn to feed the animals before the light failed altogether.

Back in the house, I opened cans of green beans and

mushrooms and put them together in a pan to heat, while Mom cooked noodles and made gravy from the juices in the roasting pan. I sliced bread and dipped icy cold water from the water barrel for us to drink. I set the fat orange candle on the table and lit it and we sat down to a wonderful dinner.

As we ate, I felt the house shake as though a blast of wind had hit it. No wind was blowing, however. The shaking continued for a few seconds. "Earthquake," Dad said quietly. By the time we realized what it was, the shaking stopped. We were used to feeling light tremors fairly often. The coast along the southern part of Alaska—the Alaska Peninsula—and the Aleutian chain of islands are located along a huge fault line in the earth's crust. The movement of two plates of the crust grinding against each other far under the surface causes many earthquakes and lots of volcanic activity. Most of the quakes cause no damage, but everyone in Alaska remembers the terrible Good Friday earthquake of 1964, which destroyed several coastal towns and changed the appearance of downtown Anchorage. Tidal waves were responsible for much of the destruction of the towns on the coast. We knew that if there were a bad earthquake we should quickly gather survival gear and food and climb the mountain to Long Jake's cabin.

After dessert of molasses crinkles and hot tea, I washed the dishes and Daddy dried them and put them away. "We haven't played a game together for a while," I suggested. "Now that we've finished reading A Walk Across America let's play a game tonight."

"Okay, what will it be?" Dad asked.

"Well, I don't feel like doing a lot of thinking tonight. Let's play a game of luck, like Thousand Aces or Yatzee."

We ended up playing several games of Thousand Aces and eating popcorn before bedtime. I even managed to win twice in a row. I usually take so many risks that don't work out that I get way behind. But this time I seemed to have a magic touch. It was fun.

Before we went to bed, Dad filled the stove with wood and turned down the damper so it would burn slowly all night. I washed my face and brushed my teeth. Dreading the cold, I took the work area lamp and hurried up the stairs to my room. I hung the lamp on a hook in my ceiling and stood right over the heat grate to change into my warm flannel nightie. My room was warmer than Mom and Dad's because the stovepipe from the kitchen stove went up through my room, but I had to climb between the icy sheets all alone and lie there shivering before my body heat warmed them up. I called k.c. He came purring and climbed up on the bed. He curled up at my back. "What a nice kitty," I thought as I drifted off to sleep.

That was pretty much how our days went through November and December. The weather alternated between snowstorms and sunshine or dull gray days. In December the temperature slid down below zero and stayed down for two weeks. We made several holes in the wall between the water barrel and the chicken pen so that the heat from the kerosene heater could go through. The other animals had grown heavy winter coats and took the cold in stride. Ice formed on the water in the inlet and the channel between us and the mainland, but the constant movement of the tide prevented it from becoming a solid sheet. Instead ice floes ground against each other and moved in and out with the tide. At low tide large chunks of ice were left on the beach and the tide flats.

For Thanksgiving we fixed a special dinner, a moose

roast cooked with potatoes and onions, green beans and mushrooms baked with cream of mushroom soup and topped with Chinese noodles, Jell-o salad with mixed fruit, cornmeal rolls, and a lovely pumpkin pie. After dinner we sang together for a long time from our hymnbook. It was a good day to sing hymns of thanks and praise.

Each week on Saturday morning we talked to Grandpa and Grandma on the CB radio, unless the weather was so bad that it ruined our reception. They were definitely planning to charter a helicopter and spend five days with us at Christmas. Uncle Greg and his wife and Uncle Kent were coming too. Aunt Rose had met a young man at college and decided to go home with him for Christmas. I was really disgusted with her for that. After we'd made a pact not to get married, at least for a long time, here she was going home with a guy for Christmas. If she was that serious, who knew what it would lead to?

After the cold snap in December, the temperature went up into the twenties and it snowed for a week off and on. The snow in the woods was so deep we couldn't get around in it except on skis or snowshoes. We all had cross-country skis, but we had only one pair of snowshoes.

On a sunny day a week before Christmas Dad put on the snowshoes and headed into the woods with Mom and me skiing behind him. Since none of us were experts with either snowshoes or skis, we floundered around and fell frequently. Soon we were covered with snow and laughing so hard we could hardly keep going. We looked for a small spruce tree to cut for Christmas. The snow was so deep we would actually be cutting only the top of a bigger tree. After a half hour of falling, laughing, and general hilarity, we found the perfect little tree. I held onto it while Dad sawed through the trunk right at the snow line and then he put it over his shoulder for the trek back. We managed to get back to the cabin without any more falls. Our faces were red with exertion and fresh, cold air, and my lungs and brain felt all cleaned out and refreshed.

We put the tree in a bucket of water in the entry hall to thaw. Mom and I unpacked the small box of Christmas things she had brought from Anchorage. Christmas wouldn't have seemed right without the wooden carving of the holy family with all the little bone china animals gathered around it to worship the Christ child. I knew that when Mom and Dad were first married and were poor college students, Mom found a very inexpensive plaster figure of the holy family to set up in their little apartment. On an inspiration she grouped her little bone china animal figures around it, a little walrus family, a bull moose, two tiny husky dogs, and a family of polar bears. That nativity scene became a tradition. Before I was born she found the wooden carving, and over the years we had added more little animals, all of them from the northland. I couldn't remember a Christmas without the animal nativity scene. When I was little I couldn't keep from picking up the little animals and rearranging them frequently. I liked to put the baby animals right up close to the baby in the manger.

The tree ornaments Mom had brought were the ones she had collected over the years to represent something special from each year since she and Dad were married. A small brass bell with the word "sweethearts" carved on it stood for the year Mom and Dad were married. There was a little mortar board for the year they graduated from college and a pink plastic baby rattle for the year I was born. An Alaska flag represented the year we moved to Alaska, a little wooden horse stood for the year I got Kenai, and a small silver fish for last year, when we had started fishing. For this year Dad had worked for several afternoons building a tiny replica of the Snuggery.

I set up the nativity scene on the little table between Mom and Dad's chairs in the living area. When the tree was thawed out we set it just behind that table so that it stood right in the middle of the living/work area. We hung all the eighteen "year" ornaments on it, then added little snail shells of all shapes and sizes that Mom and I had collected from the beach in the summer. Since we had no lights we tied red and yellow ribbon bows on the end of each branch for color. On the top we put the star of various yellow calico prints that Mom had pieced and quilted years ago. Then we all stood back to admire the beautiful little tree. A warm feeling welled up in my chest.

I love Christmas, when we celebrate how much God loves us. It's hard to believe that God actually became a man so that we could understand how much he loves us. I love Christmas because it celebrates that kind of love. We share the love by giving gifts and decorating the house and getting together with family and friends. I like the family traditions that go with Christmas—hanging the same orna-ments on the tree year after year, putting up the animal nativity scene, singing special songs, and reading the Christmas story from the Bible by candlelight on Christmas Eve.

Mom and I baked lots of cookies. Sand tarts are another tradition for Christmas at our house. We made sand tart stars and bells so thin and light they melted in our mouths. We baked ginger cookies and nutty little peppernuts and apricot-oatmeal bars. It was easy to freeze them by storing them in the entry porch.

But the real excitement was knowing that Grandpa and

Grandma, Greg and Karen and Kent were coming. They planned to arrive two days before Christmas. The day before that Dad and I walked among the ice floes on the beach down to the point and with the snowshoes we tramped down the snow and marked out a flat area where the helicopter could land. The weather was colder again and the sky was clear and showed no signs of bad weather moving in. On our way back from the point, Dad and I stopped at the fishing cabin and took three mattresses off the beds. We put them on the big cart to haul them to the house. We put two of them up in my room for Greg and Karen to sleep on. Uncle Kent would use my bed. The third mattress we put in Mom and Dad's room where I would sleep on the floor. Mom and I made up the sofa bed in the living area for Grandpa and Grandma. We brought extra bedding from the fishing cabin and opened our sleeping bags to air out.

I could hardly contain my excitement. I danced out to exercise Kenai and feed all the stock singing "Joy to the World" at the top of my lungs. At dinner I bubbled and babbled until Mom said, "Melanie, I believe we'll have to knock you out to get you to sleep tonight. You're rocking the whole house!"

"I'm so excited. We haven't seen anyone but each other for four whole months! I know Grandma will want to go for good long walks with me, and Grandpa will want to ride Kenai and I'll get to know Aunt Karen better and Uncle Greg will play Monopoly with me—he likes to play Monopoly and you two only play because you know I want to—and Uncle Kent will turn me upside down and be punny and we'll be able to sing and sound really good and play games that require more than three players and...." I ran out of steam.

"It *is* exciting," Mom said. "When you've been this isolated, company seems marvelous. But it's a little frightening, too. Will I be able to stand to have so many people, even people I love so much, around? Will I be able to talk intelligently anymore? Maybe we've turned a little crazy in the last four months and don't even know it. But I am looking forward to putting a big jigsaw puzzle together with Dad and Kent. That's one thing I always look forward to doing at Christmastime."

"Well, you may put puzzles together to your heart's content, Annie," Dad smiled at her, "as long as you don't expect me to help you. That's one thing I never could stand to do. It takes so long to make any progress. I'm looking forward to playing some Rook."

"One thing we must do is enjoy each moment no matter what we are doing," Mom pointed out. "Sometimes when we are looking forward to a special occasion we have so many expectations that we end up feeling let down instead of refreshed. I have an idea for right now. When we have finished the dishes, let's take a walk under the stars and sing Christmas carols. You may bring the animals along if you want, Melanie."

"Oh, I'd love it!" I cried. "I'll wash and you dry, Dad, and Mom can put away leftovers and clean up the kitchen."

In no time at all we were walking down the beach in the starlight, singing. I led Kenai, the goats crowded around us, the dogs ran in circles sniffing and marking ice floes and driftwood, and even k.c. brought up the rear. He meowed and complained about being cold and getting left behind. The stars twinkled through pinholes in the black velvet sky stretched from mountain to mountain. Our voices faded quickly into the crisp, cold air. As we walked toward the point, a translucent curtain of pale green light rose into the sky from behind Mount Redoubt. Higher and higher it climbed, stretching and bending and folding. "Look!" Dad pointed between phrases of "It Came Upon the Midnight Clear" and we slowed down, gazing in wonder at the northern lights. Slowly the light moved up toward the zenith, then fingers of light reached up from every direction and converged at the top of the heavens, where they formed a moving flower of light reaching down toward the horizon in long points and folds. As we watched the colors changed from pale green to rose and palest yellow. They grew so bright the stars dimmed and they seemed to pulsate to the rhythm of our songs. Without realizing it we stopped walking to turn our faces upward. I reached for Daddy's hand and was glad to feel his strong mittened hand around mine. The lights were so ethereal, so mysterious, I felt almost afraid of them. Yet I know that the lights, like our songs, and the shining stars, and the still, frozen earth, were a way of praising God. His own creation was giving him glory.

The last note of "The Message" slipped away and we stood silently together, the animals and our little family, watching the lights until they faded and our cheeks and noses felt like blocks of ice. "Wasn't that beautiful?" Mom whispered as she turned back toward the cove. We walked quietly down the beach. Even the animals walked with dignity. A great glow of joy spread out inside my soul. Thank you, God!

Chapter Six

GRANDPA AND GRANDMA, Uncle Kent, and Uncle Greg and Aunt Karen arrived two days before Christmas. They had to charter a large helicopter to carry so many people. As soon as I heard it far in the distance I ran pell-mell down to the point. The pilot came in low across the ice-choked channel and set the noisy, vibrating copter down right on target. I could hardly breathe, I was so excited.

As the blades slowed down, Uncle Kent jumped out from the passenger side and suddenly we were all hugging and laughing together in a big knot of people. The poor pilot must have felt very left out! After everyone had hugged all around, Grandma and I stood with our arms around each other while Dad and Uncle Kent helped the pilot unload their luggage and a large number of boxes and bags. "It's good we had to come in a large helicopter," Grandpa laughed, "to handle all this extra stuff your grandma insisted on bringing."

"Oh, what did you bring?" I squeezed Grandma and practically jumped up and down. "Dad said you weren't to bring any Christmas presents, because this is present enough. It is, too!"

"Well, I couldn't resist a few little things." Grandma's eyes twinkled at me. "And some fresh produce—vegetables and fruit. I knew you'd enjoy that."

I had been secretly hoping Grandma would bring along fresh apples and oranges and things for salad. "Oh, Grandma!" I exclaimed, hugging her again, "You couldn't have brought anything better. Oh, I can't wait to eat an orange!"

Mom hugged her too. "I've been craving a nice green salad. Thank you! Let's help get everything into the cabin before all that good stuff freezes."

The cart was soon full of goodies. We all backed away as the pilot started the helicopter and took off. He circled over us and headed back toward the forelands.

"Well, now we know what it's like to be left alone on an island," Uncle Greg said. "There goes our only possible means of transportation."

I didn't bother to get Kenai to pull the cart back to the house. There were so many people we took turns pulling it along the upper edge of the beach where the water had washed away the snow but left a few ice floes.

Uncle Kent had helped build the Snuggery, but the others hadn't seen it at all. They exclaimed about how nice it looked from the outside, and when everyone had removed boots and coats and all the accessories in the crowded little entry hall, they exclaimed about how cozy and pleasant it was inside. With five extra people the little house suddenly seemed very full, but it was lovely to look around and see all their dear faces. Grandpa stood by the wood stove warming his hands. Uncle Greg sat on the couch with his arm around Karen. This was their first Christmas since they were married, although Greg isn't very much younger than Mom. He and Karen were married in the spring, shortly before we left for the island. Uncle Kent was checking out the bookshelves and the view from the windows. All of a sudden he turned around and grabbed me. "It's been far too long since I've turned you upside down," he laughed, and next thing there I was, viewing the kitchen, where Mom and Grandma were putting away the goodies, upside down.

"Hold on a minute, Kent," Dad told him. "I don't often get an opportunity like this," and he gave me a little spank. "That should keep you on good behavior for at least the next six months, Melanie."

"Oh, Daddy! Let me down, Kent. I think my head's beginning to swell from all the blood running into it."

"Ha! Your head was already swelled," Uncle Kent joked as he set me back on my feet.

Grandma gave me an orange. "Now let Melanie alone so she can enjoy this orange. She hasn't had one in four months."

"Oooh, Grandma!" I squealed. "It looks delicious, it smells delicious, it even feels delicious!"

I got a knife and carefully cut the orange into twelve wedges, put them on a plate, and sat down at the table to savor them. Dad sat down, too. "May I have some, Melanie?"

"You may have one of your own, Charlie," Grandma scolded him with a smile. "I brought half a box of them because they'll keep for a while, and I knew all of us would want some over Christmas."

The orange was sweet and tangy, absolutely luscious. I ate the white pulp off the skin, leaving only the thin orange rind that was bitter. I didn't want to waste a bit of that orange. Then everyone settled in for a long morning of talking. We told all about our various adventures, trying not to make them sound too serious so Grandma and Grandpa wouldn't worry about us. They told us about what was happening in Homer and Anchorage and the world in general. At lunchtime, Dad brought in a piece of plywood that he had cut from a piece left over from building and put it over the table to make it bigger. I covered it with a large yellow tablecloth and set the table while Mom and Dad warmed up the big pot of chili and baked corn muffins. Dad sliced up some carrots and celery Grandma had brought. We kept right on talking through the meal and most of the afternoon.

Finally it was time for me to feed the animals, and Dad exclaimed, "Oh, I meant to fill the water barrel a long time ago!" Uncle Kent went out to help me with my chores and say hello to Kenai and the goats and the dogs. The dogs were especially glad to see him. He knelt down to hug each one and got licked in the face and pawed all over. Uncle Greg and Grandpa helped Dad bring in blocks of snow to fill the water barrels. They cut an extra cartful and left it in the cart right outside the door so they could keep replenishing the supply as the snow melted. We needed a lot more water with eight people instead of three.

After dinner the eight of us sang all the Christmas carols we could remember. The little house rang with joy at the full, rich music of eight voices instead of three. I felt relaxed, warm, contented, and full of gladness.

Next morning was the day of Christmas Eve. There were a lot more packages under the tree than the ones we had put there. Mom had gotten all the food ready for Christmas before her family arrived, so we had a lovely day to do other things. It was clear and bright and the temperature was in the upper teens, a good day to go outdoors. Uncle Greg and Karen decided to take a walk around the point and explore in that direction. Uncle Kent and Dad went out to go over the generator and other things that Uncle Kent's mechanic ability was good for, and Mom and Grandpa and Grandma and I decided to ski up to Long Jake's cabin. We hadn't gone up there since October when we had to get water from the spring.

The path was deeply buried with snow but I was sure I could find the way. We let the dogs loose and I wished I could take Kenai along, but I was afraid he would sink into the drifts. It took some work to get up some of the steeper places on the trail, but we all managed. In about an hour and a half we arrived in the clearing. The tiny cabin was all but covered with snow. Without a shovel, we couldn't even open the door; it was drifted shut. When Long Jake lived there he must have had to work hard keeping an open path between the cabin and the barn and out to the spring. We skied along the trail to the spring and sure enough it was still running. There was a great mound of ice over it and water seeped out from under it, freezing quickly and making the glacier ever bigger. Probably Long Jake kept that ice cut away so that he could get water all winter.

In spite of being bundled in wool scarves and caps and ski gloves, our faces and hands began to get cold, so we headed back down the trail again. Of course we made much better time going downhill on a trail that was already marked. We arrived back at the house at about the same time as Greg and Karen. Our cheeks and noses were bright red, but we felt refreshed and energetic as we trooped into the entry way and removed our boots and coats and extra layers of clothes. Dad and Uncle Kent had fixed potato soup and peanut butter muffins for lunch. We topped it off with shiny red apples, then relaxed and talked over tea and cookies.

In the afternoon Mom and Grandpa started their puzzle. They did it on the table. At mealtime we could just put the plywood over it and eat without disturbing the puzzle. I thought that was a clever idea. Dad and Uncle Kent spent the afternoon reading, and Uncle Greg and Karen and I played Monopoly. It turned out that Karen was a Monopoly fan, too. I guess that's one of the things she and Greg liked about each other. I enjoyed getting to know Karen better. She is a secretary in a private medical clinic. She likes to fly as a hobby and that's how she met Uncle Greg, who teaches flying. They both like outdoor activities a lot. They met on a fly-in wilderness camping trip. They fly all over the state to go camping or hiking or skiing, even in the winter time. But when he's not outdoors or flying Uncle Greg likes to play games, especially Monopoly. Mom says that when he was a boy he played Monopoly against himself if he couldn't get anyone to play with him. We had a good long game that afternoon. I went bankrupt first, although I hung on for a long time with just the red monopoly and two railroads. Karen got all my property when I landed on her hotel on North Carolina Avenue. So she had an advantage and eventually she wiped out Uncle Greg, too. By then it was dark outdoors and we played by lamplight.

I had to go out to feed the animals. This time Grandpa helped. It was fun to have someone to enjoy the animals with me. Kenai likes Grandpa, and Grandpa understands a lot of what Kenai has to say, so they had a little talk while I took care of the chickens and the goats. The dogs were tired from their morning's romp. They came reluctantly out of their houses to eat their dinner. On our way back to the house Grandpa and I stood still and looked up into the starry sky.

"You know, Melanie," Grandpa said. "I often look up at the sky at night and know that you and Anne and Charlie can see the same sky from here. Somehow that makes me feel better. Even though we seem to be so isolated from each other we are still together here on God' earth. How do you feel about being on Gresham Island by now?"

"Oh, I really like it, Grandpa. Sometimes I miss having friends around my own age, especially when Mom and Dad are bugging me, but I guess I'm sort of a loner anyhow. As long as I can have Kenai and the dogs and other animals to spend time with I'm fine. I like not having to depend on anyone else and not feeling obligated to look after my friends when they've got problems and stuff. I think I could probably live alone all the time, like Long Jake did."

"Even Long Jake needed other people," Grandpa said softly, almost to himself. "He just didn't know it until you came along."

"Well, I'm glad you came for Christmas, Grandpa. And I'm glad we can talk to you on the CB every week. It is a good feeling to know that you and Grandma and the aunts and uncles and everyone miss us and think about us. I miss you, too. I guess we'd better go in now. Dinner should soon be ready."

If someone were to ask me what I like best about Christmas, I would have to say that it really isn't Christmas morning when we open our gifts, although that is a very exciting time. My favorite part is Christmas Eve. After dinner, while Grandma and Karen did the dishes, Mom and I lit every candle in the house. We lit one kerosene lamp, too, to read by, but when the dishes were done we turned out the gas lamps. The candles flickered and made warm shadows on the walls; the room felt warm and cozy and quiet. We sang. We started with "O Come All Ye Faithful," "Joy to the World," and "The Message," a special carol that Grandma and Grandpa had learned when they were young. Then, by candlelight, Grandpa read the Christmas story from Luke 2 and Dad read the story of the wise men from Matthew.

I have heard those passages many, many times, but when we read them on Christmas Eve in the candlelight I get goose pimples, they're so beautiful. I can picture the stable where Jesus was born, with inquisitive animals looking on, and the barn smell and sounds. I can hear the angel making his announcement to the shepherds and the joyful music of the choir. I can feel the excitement of the shepherds and their confusion. I'm sure they didn't really understand much that happened that night. Probably nobody did, but they knew it was somehow a world-shaking event. Mom has always explained to me that Jesus' coming was sort of like God speaking our language so that we could understand how much he loves us and why he made us. God's own language is so fantastically beyond our comprehension that he decided to explain his love in a way we can understand. It's absolutely amazing!

After the reading we sang again, "In a Lowly Little Manger," which is another special song Grandma learned as a young girl, and "Silent Night." That was the part of the celebration that is the same every year. When Mom was a girl they had two angel candles that her aunt gave to her and her sister. Aunt Teresa now lives with her family in Colorado. They always lit just those two candles while they read the Christmas story and Mom and Aunt Terry sang "In a Lowly Little Manger." The angel candles finally burned away but the tradition still goes on. In fact, we knew that Aunt Terry's family was celebrating the same way in Colorado, and if Aunt Rose could, she would probably try to celebrate Christmas Eve with her boyfriend by reading Luke 2 by candlelight.

Usually, after the candlelight celebration we all go caroling for friends and neighbors, but since there were no friends and neighbors on Gresham Island, we bundled up and went out to sing for the animals and then just stood under the stars and sang for God. When we went back in the house we did the part of the celebration that comes from Dad's family. We had hot chocolate and birthday cake for Jesus' birthday. Mom brought out a lovely carrot cake with cream cheese icing and a candle for each century since Jesus' birth and we sang "Happy Birthday, dear Jesus," and blew out the candles.

Then it was bedtime and Christmas morning came quickly. I got up and went out into the cold with a lantern, to feed the animals. I gave them all special treats for Christmas. Kenai got a carrot, the goats got turnips Grandma had brought especially for them, and the chickens got some real corn. I gave Talkie and Goofus each a rawhide bone.

Then I hurried indoors, where the fire was crackling and Mom had steaming cups of coffee and tea for everyone and delicious sweet rolls to enjoy while we opened gifts. My favorite gifts were books: *A Guide to Birds of Alaska, The Complete Poems of Emily Dickinson,* and three of James

Michener's long novels to keep me busy: *Chesapeake*, *Centenniel*, and *The Covenant*. Grandma gave me a lovely stuffed mallard duck she made herself and Mom had made a beautiful patchwork vest in shades of blue. It had embroidery and small appliquéd designs on the crazy patches. "I think it will fit you for a long time so you can wear it to school when we move back to town," Mom said.

All the gifts I gave were handmade but everyone seemed to enjoy them. I made driftwood mobiles for Grandpa and Grandma and Uncle Greg and Karen. For Dad I did a counted cross-stitch pillow top with fish on it and I also did one for Kent with a little blue and yellow airplane like his Champ. Mom had been the hardest person to make something for, because she makes so many neat things herself, but I finally took some of the best shells I had collected during the summer and combined them with some small pieces of driftwood to make a mobile.

For Christmas dinner we had a turkey that Grandma had brought, a real tossed salad with homemade French dressing, clam stuffing, and creamed peas with mushrooms. For dessert Mom brought out mince pie, which is Dad's favorite and liked by everyone except me. But she had made a chocolate cream pie for me. How delightful!

The rest of the visit sped by. The weather stayed clear with temperatures in the teens; we took walks every day. Grandpa even rode Kenai while I led him along the trail we had made at the top of the beach. My sweet little Grandma walked with me all the way to the fossil rocks on the other side of the island one day. I told her what I was doing for schoolwork and how I had decided I'd like to be a writer like Mom someday.

"I think you will make a good writer," Grandma told me. "You have a vivid imagination. You should be especially good at writing animal stories. I suspect you could write a story where the animals talk and so forth while still retaining their animal characteristics, like *Watership Down*, because you have the ability to communicate with your pets."

"Sometimes I think I communicate better with my pets than I do with most people. My friends back in Anchorage often don't make sense to me at all, or else they spend all their time talking about boys and clothes and their favorite rock stars." It was easy to talk to Grandma. "I guess they think I'm weird because I like to talk about animals and how to train them. Or I want to talk about how to get along with other people, or why I get so bugged by my mother. I just have different interests than most girls my age. I really don't miss those kids nearly as much as I thought I would."

"But you'd probably enjoy having someone your own age to interact with sometimes, wouldn't you? Don't you find it hard to be stuck here on the island with just your parents?"

"Well, yes, in fact sometimes they bug me so much I just have to get away from them for a while. It's crazy; it's just little things that annoy me, like Mom's irregular typing when she's writing. Or when she makes a big deal out of some small thing Dad or I do that bugs her. And I can't stand to hear her sing tunes without words but she does it all the time."

"We all are irritated by little things," Grandma replied. "I guess it's even more so when you are isolated in close quarters. I remember when your mother was your age and we lived in a small Eskimo village. We all went a little stir-crazy by late winter, February and March. Your mother was bugged by things I did then, just the same sorts of things, so she probably understands how you feel. But you

101

probably drive her batty sometimes, too."

"Oh, I'm sure I do. One thing that helps is that Mom saw to it that we all take some private time for an hour after lunch every day. But I guess getting irritated with Mom and Dad is the only bad thing about being on the island. I get so tired of parents sometimes. It's really nice to have you here for these few days. But you know, Grandma, I feel very capable of being here alone and most of the time I really enjoy it."

"Yes, I'm sure you do, Melanie," Grandma gave me a quick squeeze. "I've been thinking of you and Anne and Charlie every day and praying for you. I have every confidence that you'll continue to have a good winter."

A raven croaked from the top of a tree up on the bank. A couple of ravens were the only big birds left on the island in the middle of the winter. Even the eagles had gone to find a place where food was more plentiful. The ravens liked dog food, I discovered, and they spent a lot of time foraging in the pile of discarded bedding from Kenai's and the goats' stalls. They also liked to follow us on our walks, making comical raven comments as they flew from tree to tree with great dignity. The thing about ravens is that they try so hard to be dignified when in fact they are generally quite silly. This raven sounded so serious that Grandma and I burst out laughing. I love to laugh with Grandma. When something strikes her funny she giggles until the tears come, and it's contagious. Everyone else always ends up giggling with her. So that was the end of our serious conversation for that day.

Grandpa and Mom finished their 2,500-piece puzzle; we all played many games and sang together. On the sixth morning they all packed up their things and we put them in the cart. It wasn't nearly as full as it had been when they arrived. Before long we heard the helicopter coming toward the island and we hurried up to the point. All the hugging happened again, as the pilot helped Kent and Greg stow the baggage. Then everyone climbed into the copter and off it went. We waved and waved and we could see Grandma waving from her seat beside the pilot. They circled over us to gain altitude and then headed north over the ice floes. For some reason we stood together there on the point until we could no longer hear the faintest hum of the helicopter. Usually the air was filled with the sounds of bird noises, grinding ice, lapping water, and the creaks and groans of the cold earth. Suddenly there was a broad silence. I felt tiny, a little speck standing on the snow with two other specks in a white silent world.

I'm so glad they came," Mom's voice sounded loud in the quiet. "It made Christmas special, and it gave us a good break from each other and our routine."

"Yes, it certainly was fun to have them," Dad said as he picked up the tongue of the cart and began to pull it back down the beach.

"I loved having them here!" I exclaimed. "But I know we *could* have had a good Christmas without them if they hadn't come." It seemed necessary to point out that we could take care of ourselves.

"Of course we could have, but we didn't need to. Having the family here was a refreshing change and I feel more able to face the next couple of months because of it. All the fresh produce certainly was a pleasure, too. I'm so glad my mother insisted on bringing it," Mom smiled.

We walked slowly back to the cabin, dragging the empty cart. Mom and I spent the rest of the morning house cleaning while Dad filled the water barrel with snow blocks and split wood. In the afternoon we heated water and

103

melted snow in a huge old copper boiler and washed clothes and bedding in the gas washing machine on the porch. We hung the bedding out in the freezing air to dry. Of course it froze immediately but the damp evaporated out in the breeze. When we brought in the wash we hung it on a rack near the cookstove to finish drying overnight. The sheets and towels smelled fresh and clean from being out in the clear air. Even though my fingers nearly froze when I hung the things outdoors I always felt it was worth it later when I folded them and they smelled so good.

Already we were past the shortest day of the year, December 21, but the days don't seem to lengthen much through January, and that is always a time when you must work to keep your spirits up in Alaska. We woke up and ate breakfast in the dark. We worked by lamplight because even when the sun did rise around 10:00 it hung so low in the sky that it was behind the island mountain most of the day. It set again around 3:00 in a blaze of glory behind Mt. Illiamna. We often took time from our chores to ski across the point toward Hanson's cabin and watch it. But there were many days when the sun didn't show through the clouds and wind and snow. The wind often blew so fiercely we hurried through our outdoor chores as fast as we could and were glad to be back inside the cozy house again. I know the animals were glad for their snug barn, too.

We had asked Grandpa to bring us a big supply of extra batteries for our radio, so we didn't skimp on listening to programs from Homer's public radio station. Playing classical or folk music made a pleasant background to work by. But in spite of all our efforts, I found I got irritated very easily. Sometimes I would get into a shouting match with Mom. Afterward I felt rotten and nasty and I often ran up-stairs to sob on my bed. Or I would just get so fed up with trying to reason with Dad that I flung out of the house in total sullen silence and took Kenai or the dogs for a walk. That happened most often when he was trying to explain my math to me and it seemed to me he was being extremely obtuse. When I finally sneaked guiltily back into the house Dad acted like nothing had happened. He asked me how Kenai was and Mom suggested I bake some cookies. I guess they got their feelings out with each other while I was gone and forgave me, but I had a hard time feeling forgiven.

Chapter Seven

ONE OF THE GOATS, Isabella, was due to kid in January. I began to watch her closely. We wanted to put her in a separate stall all by herself when the time came. But somehow I missed the signs, because one morning I went out to the barn and there was Isabella in a corner of the main stall, proudly licking a tiny black and white kid. He was perfectly formed and marked, all black with white outlines—white on the edges of his ears, white fringes on his tiny tail, and white ankles—but he was extremely small. I was surprised because Isabella had been so very big.

Then I saw two other little kids lying nearby. One was still covered by the sac he was born in and he was dead. I thought the other was dead, too, but she opened her tiny mouth and "maa-aa-ed" feebly. Her nose and mouth were licked clean, but apparently Isabella had abandoned her when the little black one was born. Now she lay on her side in the cold, cold barn. In an instant I snatched her up, hurried to the feed room, and wrapped a feed sack around her. I carried her tenderly into the house.

"Oh, Mom and Dad, look at this! Isabella had triplets and one is dead and this one is almost gone. What can we do?"

Dad took a look and took charge. "We have to get her warm and get some milk into her. What a thin little kid! Her legs are like pencils. Here, Melanie, let's put her right beside the stove. Annie, may we have a box and some rags? I think we'll need to rub her down to simulate her mother's licking. That's what usually gets a baby goat's circulation going so it will stand up."

While Mom looked for an old blanket, I knelt beside the stove with the tiny kid in my arms and began stroking her back. She felt cold as ice and I was sure her thin little legs must be frozen. But she looked around and maa-aa-ed feebly again as I petted her. Unlike the beautiful kid still in the barn with Belle, this kid was gray with dark gray spots scattered unevenly over her body. Her coat had not been licked clean and smooth like his; she looked pathetic. I fell in love with her immediately!

Mom brought an old wool blanket and held it close to the stove to warm it up. "Hold her close to you, Melanie," she advised. "Your body heat will be the best way to warm her up. And keep stroking her to get the circulation going." She put the blanket down and began to rub the tiny legs. "When I was in the feed store buying things to bring for this winter I thought of this possibility and bought a nipple to use on a catsup bottle or something. Now I'll have to figure out where I put it."

"Oh, Mom, just look how tiny she is," I breathed. "Her

107

little hooves aren't any bigger than the end of my finger. And see how spunky she is? She is watching you. I think she's going to make it because she's so determined to live."

Dad had hurried out to check on Belle and the other kid. He returned and sat down on the hallway bench to take off his boots. "Isabella and the other kid seem to be doing fine. I moved them into the little stall by themselves and put the dead kid in a feed bag in the feed room. We'll have to wait until spring to bury it. Anyway, I don't think the other little fellow will get too cold. He's moving around and drinking milk and staying close to Belle. She seems to have plenty of milk. How's this little one doing?"

"Oh, Daddy, she's so spunky and cute. Look how tiny she is. I think she's beginning to get warm."

"Well, we need to milk Isabella right away and get some warm milk into her. And we need to get her to stand up. She won't make it if she doesn't soon stand on her own. Annie, where's a bucket? I need to milk Belle." Dad knelt beside me to feel the little kid's legs. "That's good, Melanie. Just keep stroking her pretty firmly and rub her legs. Tuck this warm blanket around her and stay right close to the stove so she gets warmed up as fast as possible."

Mom came out of the pantry with a little plastic bucket in one hand and the nipple in the other. "Here's the nipple. I think I have an empty catsup bottle to put it on. Do you need help to milk Isabella, Charlie?"

"Belle's used to being milked," Dad replied as he pulled his boots back on. "I'm sure I can do it myself." He took the bucket and went out the door.

I cuddled the little kid and stroked her. I could tell she was getting warm as she stopped shivering and seemed to curl up against me. When Dad came back in with the

108

bucket half full of milk, Mom had the bottle ready. She put a little milk into it and warmed it up in a pan of hot water. Then Dad brought it and tried to feed the little goat. She seemed interested as milk dripped over her tiny nose and she licked it but she wouldn't open her mouth to take the nipple. Dad dipped his finger in some milk in a bowl and pushed his finger into the little mouth, forcing it open. She licked eagerly at his finger. Her tiny tail wagged weakly. When Dad tried to stick the nipple in her mouth again, she took it and licked at it but didn't seem to know how to suck. Dad worked the nipple around in her mouth and she kept swallowing as milk dribbled down her throat. Then she began to suck noisily. Suddenly her tail bobbed furiously the way all baby goats' tails do when they are happily being fed.

"Oh, good," Dad echoed my feelings. "Now if we can just get her to stand up on her own, she'll be okay."

But every time we tried to help her stand up, those pencil-thin legs collapsed underneath her and she fell in an awkward heap. As the day passed we let her sleep on the blanket by the stove, fed her, and stroked her. She seemed interested in her surroundings and took her bottle eagerly, but she just couldn't control those legs. "When she learns to stand," Dad said, "we'll take her back out to Isabella and hope she accepts her. She'll be better off if she can be with her own mother."

"But won't she get too cold out there?" I asked.

"If she can move around on her own, she should stay warm with Belle and the other kid," Dad said. "The little buck is doing fine."

By evening she still wasn't standing and I felt discouraged. I felt sad as I sat on the floor beside her while Mom read to us from *All Creatures Great and Small,* by

James Herriott, the veterinarian. It seemed an appropriate book to be reading, but I thought, "James Herriott would have her standing by now, and here we don't know what to do."

Dad sat in his chair on the other side of the kid and kept prodding her with his toe, pushing under her belly like her mother might do with her nose to get a reluctant kid to stand. She would manage to get her back legs up but the front ones wouldn't cooperate. Next time she'd get the front ones up but the back ones would collapse. Dad kept prodding and she struggled and struggled. I was about ready to scold Dad for being so hard on her, when she made a mighty effort and got all four legs under her! Mom stopped reading and we all held our breath as she stood there wobbling and swaying. Then her front legs buckled and she went down, almost on her nose. But she had done it; she tried again and before long she was standing again on her thin shaky legs.

"Look at how wobbly you are," I laughed. "You're just wobbly all over. I was going to name you Spunky, but I think Wobbly will be a better name for you." She tried to come toward me and fell over in a little heap. "Yes, you're Wobbly, but I don't know what to name your beautiful brother. Maybe Little Lord Fauntleroy."

By the time we'd finished reading, Wobbly was taking a few tentative steps, and Dad felt we should take her out to the barn and at least give her a chance to have a good-night snack straight from her mother's udder. We all dressed up warmly. I carried Wobbly, wrapped in the blanket, and Dad carried a lantern. In Belle's stall Dad put Wobbly down close to her mother. The other kid was curious and came to sniff at her while Isabella stood looking on disdainfully. Little Lord Fauntleroy began to dance and jump around Wobbly, trying to get her to play. She made a few side steps in response and managed not to fall down. Dad stepped in, picked her up, and put her down at Isabella's udder. She knew what to do. She butted her little head into her mother's udder, grabbed a teat, and began to suck while her little tail wagged like mad.

Isabella turned her head to look and sniff, then lowered her head and butted little Wobbly right off her feet! And that was that. No matter if we held Belle's head so she couldn't butt her daughter while she drank, she kicked her instead. She seemed determined to have nothing to do with that little goat!

"What kind of mother are you?" I asked Belle sternly. "Wobbly needs you!" But secretly I was kind of glad to think that now I would have to be Wobbly's mother.

We carried her back into the house and put her in a box in the hallway for the night. In the middle of the night I woke up to the sound of pitiful little bleats from the bottom of the stairs. I got up in the cold night, lit a lantern, heated a little milk on the stove, and fed Wobbly, who stood up in her box and drank while her tail wriggled with satisfaction.

So Wobbly became part of the family. We milked Isabella every morning and evening and she still had plenty of milk for Little Lord Roy, who grew fat and sleek. His black coat glistened and he loved to jump and butt and do cute things. He liked to play with Wobbly and she enjoyed playing with him but we had to let them play away from their mother because she would wallop Wobbly whenever she got too close to her udder. We got a larger box for Wobbly and she stayed in the house most of the time, but whenever I took her along outdoors she followed me like a puppy. She continued to look wobbly. Her coat was rough and uneven. Her back was humped. She was anything but graceful. At the slightest bump she fell over or stumbled. But I loved her and she loved me.

The problems came as she grew bigger. The problems weren't with Wobbly; they were with Mom. From the time Wobbly was about a week old, at least once a day Mom would say, "We need to get Wobbly acclimated to being outdoors. She'll soon be too big to stay in the house. She's making it stink in here already."

That irritated me so much. Here was a little goat whose mother didn't want it. I was willing to put up with a little smell and to clean up a few messes now and then for the sake of a poor motherless goat. It was too cold to make her stay outdoors all the time. Besides, the other goats might be mean to Wobbly and she was too little and awkward to defend herself. But my mother had no sympathy. She said she did. She'd say, "It will be the best thing for Wobbly to stay out with the other goats as soon as possible. If you love her you want to do what's best for her." So every day we'd have a big argument. I told Mom how unsympathetic and mean and cruel she was, and she insisted that Wobbly be kept outdoors more. So I took Wobbly out to the barn and put her in with the other goats for a little while, but I went out to check on her within an hour and she was always in some kind of trouble so I brought her back in.

By the time she was two weeks old, Wobbly didn't have to be fed nearly so often and she was jumping out of any box we put her in. She would jump out and come right to me. She'd nuzzle her head up under my hand so I would scratch the place where her tiny horns were growing and she stayed close to me wherever I went. If I was doing my schoolwork she lay down beside me and I petted her every once in a while but she didn't bother me. But Mom said she was interrupting my schoolwork. Mom harped on the idea that the house was getting stinky. She got really upset when she found goat droppings or puddles on the floor even though I cleaned them up right away. One day Wobbly chewed a hole in the quilt Mom kept on her rocker to use as an afghan. Mom got unreasonable.

"The goat is going to have to start being a goat and stay in the barn," she shouted. "This is the last straw! I won't put up with her in the house any longer. She is perfectly capable of staying in the barn."

"But, Mom, you didn't make me move out to the barn when I wet my pants or crayoned on the wall. Wobbly is just like a baby. She needs understanding and love and attention."

"Wobbly is not a baby—she's a goat. She behaves like a goat and she needs to know she's a goat. You can give her all the understanding and love and attention she needs in the barn. Besides she'll have fun playing with Little Lord Roy and the other goats. I know you love her, Melanie, and I don't want you to stop loving her. I like her, too. But she *may not* stay in the house any longer!"

I knew that when Mom got that way it was useless to argue with her. I was so mad at her and felt so powerless that I quivered inside. I turned to Dad.

"Your mom is right, Melanie. Wobbly is old enough to stay in the barn and take care of herself now. I understand how you feel, but it's just the way it is."

How could they understand how I felt? Poor rejected little Wobbly. I was the only one who loved her. What do you do when your parents are so unreasonable and stubborn and you don't have anyone else to talk to? I took Wobbly and went out to the barn and talked to Kenai. And I got an idea. I was telling Kenai that when I grew up and lived in my own place I wouldn't mind having animals live with me and cleaning up after them or letting them chew on things. Suddenly I realized I already had a place I could call my own—Long Jake's cabin! "I'll just move up there," I thought aloud to Kenai. "I'll take you and Wobbly and the dogs and we'll live up there. Mom and Dad can have the Snuggery to themselves!"

I hurried back into the house. "I'm going to go live in Long Jake's cabin," I told my parents. "Then Wobbly can live with me in the house and so can the dogs, and nobody will mind what they do."

"It will be a big job moving up there with all this snow on the ground," Dad said. "Are you sure that's a wise thing to do? It could get real stormy and cold and lonely."

"Well, there's plenty of wood up there. I can dig it out."

"What about Kenai? He'll miss you, but you have no way of keeping water thawed for him up there." Dad *would* think of all the obstacles.

"If I give him fresh water every couple of hours, he'll be okay," I replied. "I can keep melting snow in the cabin. Listen, I've decided this is what I'm going to do and you can't stop me. The only way I'll stay in this house is if Wobbly can stay in the house, too. Even then, I'm not sure I'd want to stay with people who can be so cruel to a poor little motherless goat."

Dad looked at Mom, who hadn't said a word. "Mel, if you think that's what you really want to do, then I guess you should give it a try. But you are going to have to be *very* careful to keep a fire going so you don't get too cold, but not to let your fire get out of control. And I insist on go-ing up to check if you're okay every day. Also, you must continue to do your schoolwork. Now, you still have time to break a trail up there before dark. Take along a shovel to dig out the wood and dig the snow away from the door. Be

114

sure to be back here by dinnertime. You can move up there tomorrow."

For some reason or other I felt a little disappointed. I guess I expected them to make more of a fuss than they did. But there was work to be done. I got the shovel and took the snowshoes down from the side of the porch. I walked down the beach to the fishing cabin, put on the snowshoes, and started along the edge of the woods to the trail to Long Jake's cabin. We'd skied it at Christmas, but I hadn't been up there since then. There was deep snow in the woods, no sign of the trail, but I knew where to go. Soon I realized that I couldn't tramp the snow down hard enough for Kenai. He would break through into snow up to his belly at every step. "So he won't be able to come," I thought. "I'll have to go down to see him every day and make sure Dad feeds him right. Oh, well, that way Dad won't have to come up to Long Jake's cabin and intrude on me there."

Mom and Dad wouldn't let me skip my schoolwork to move the next morning. Poor little Wobbly spent all night and the forenoon in the barn with the other goats. Little Lord Roy liked her and played with her. Most of the other goats ignored her, but Isabella knocked her across the room whenever she got too close. It made me feel furious.

After lunch I packed up my schoolbooks and a box of food, as well as my clothes and some bedding. I put them in our small dogsled and hitched Talkie and Goofus to it. They aren't very good sled dogs because neither one is a leader, so they spend an inordinate amount of time exploring along the trail, stopping to scratch, and so forth. But it was easier to get the stuff up the hill with them pulling erratically than me pushing alone. Wobbly wandered along with us. Occasionally I had to rescue her from a snowdrift.

Finally she got so tired that I put her on top of the pile in the sled and she rode the rest of the way. I covered her with a blanket so she wouldn't get too cold.

At the cabin I hurried to unload the sled and get a fire going in the stove. Wobbly and the dogs came indoors with me. The dogs were used to Wobbly and didn't bother her but she was curious and tried to play with them as she did with Little Lord Roy. She leaped over them and butted at them but they just lay on the floor panting and acting tolerant.

Soon the fire was crackling and the cabin grew warmer. I felt free and cozy as I put up the food, arranged my clothes on the shelf above the bed, and stacked my books on one corner of the table, where I would work. Then I found a bucket and took the animals out with me to gather snow to melt. Long Jake's water barrel was smaller than the one we had at the Snuggery but it took me a good hour to fill it with snow blocks. I put a big kettle on the stove to melt some faster to fix dinner with.

By then it was dark outdoors. The stars shone bright in a dark velvet sky so I split wood by starshine. I wanted to be sure to have enough to last the night and the next morning while I did my schoolwork. I had to make Wobbly stay in the house while I split wood because she was too curious to stay out of the way. It took at least another hour to split all that wood. I was hot and breathing heavily when I carried the last armload into the cabin. I lit the lantern, but I had to rest for a while before I started my dinner. It's hard work to live by yourself in the wilderness!

I started my routine the very next day. After breakfast I did my schoolwork. I saved questions to take to Mom or Dad after lunch when I went down the trail to see Kenai. Wobbly and the dogs went with me. I groomed Kenai and took him for a walk along the beach. Mom helped me with some Spanish conjugations, and Dad went over my math quickly. They seemed quite nice now that I didn't have to stay with them all the time. Mom was still very quiet. I suspect she didn't really approve of letting me stay at Long Jake's cabin. She always imagines that terrible things will happen. But she didn't even say anything about being careful.

I hurried back up the trail, carrying Wobbly part of the way, and got a little more snow to fill up the water barrel. Then I split wood for another hour, fixed my dinner, and spent the evening reading with Wobbly, Talkie, and Goofus lying on the floor around me. As I lay in bed trying to go to sleep I thought of my friends back in Anchorage and wondered what they would think of what I was doing. How many of them would be able to manage all by themselves like this?

A week went by. On Friday Mom and Dad invited me to have lunch with them the next day, since I wouldn't be doing schoolwork all morning. It was fun to eat someone else's cooking, although Wobbly bawled when I left her in the barn with the other goats. Mom had fixed a moose roast with gravy to put over noodles, a spinach soufflé made with canned spinach, and a blueberry pie. They were things I like but didn't know how to cook. In spite of myself I enjoyed eating that food and sitting at the table in the Snuggery talking with Mom and Dad. I hadn't realized how much fun it is to talk at the table.

When I had dinner back in my own cabin that evening it seemed very quiet. I heard myself chattering nonsense to the animals. I thought of all the long years Long Jake had lived here by himself without a soul to talk to all winter long, and for the first time I wondered how he did it. My trip down the hill to see Kenai and talk to Mom and Dad was the high point of each day. Otherwise every day seemed to be pretty much alike. I worked hard just to keep warm, have water to drink, and food to eat. I began to miss playing games with Mom and Dad in the evening and having time to do crafts and sewing and baking in the afternoons. I missed having Dad with me when I cut snow blocks and split wood as I did down at the Snuggery. I tried to persuade myself that it was just a stage I was going through, but I thought about things like that more and more often.

The dogs stayed outdoors for a large part of the day and in the lean-to at night since they were used to being out, but Wobbly stayed in the house with me all the time I was indoors. About two weeks after I had moved up to the cabin I had to write an essay for my comp course. I was writing about people's need for solitude and independence and I got very involved in it, I guess because I wanted to prove a point. I paid no attention to Wobbly, who usually lay by my chair while I worked. This morning she must have gotten bored, because I suddenly became aware of a chewing sound and turned around. There was Wobbly, standing on her hind legs with her front hooves on a shelf of the bookcase. She had pulled a book part way out and was calmly chewing away on the spine of it. With a lurch of my heart I saw that it was one of the treasured books that Long Jake had written.

"Wobbly!" I yelled. She jumped down and looked around at me innocently, her jaws still moving. I ran to her. "Wobbly, how *could* you?"

Carefully I picked up the book. It was the one about kittiwakes. The top half of the spine was all chewed away and the bound edges of the pages were ragged and wet. The

118

book was still readable, but it was ruined. I felt sick. Of all the things Long Jake had left for me, these books were the most precious because when I read them I could hear his voice telling me about the birds and animals as he used to do. As I looked at Wobbly still chomping away on a last piece of cloth binding, I realized that Mom was right. Wobbly belonged in the barn with the other goats. In this cabin I could easily clean up her messes and I didn't mind the smell all that much, but Wobbly was a herd animal and she got bored when I paid no attention to her. She had to have something to do. Since there was no Little Lord Roy to play with, she chewed things. And that could ruin even this cabin in short order.

I didn't know what to do. Wobbly was used to being in the warm house most of the time and might get sick if I penned her up in Long Jake's goat shed by herself. She would probably be all right with the other goats because all their body heat and Kenai's kept the snug barn quite warm. But how could I go down the hill and admit to Mom and Dad that they were right? I was beginning to hope they might tell me I had to move back down, but they didn't. That night I put the chairs in front of the bookcase, but I hardly slept at all. I was worried that Wobbly might chew something else. I couldn't figure out what I was going to do.

In the morning I felt very tired. My back and legs ached and my head throbbed. I could hardly get out of bed and build the fire; as soon as it was burning I crawled back under the covers until the cabin got warm. I tried to eat a little breakfast, but I couldn't concentrate on my schoolwork. Finally I went back to bed and just lay there. I forced myself to get up occasionally to feed the fire. Part of the time I shivered and then I got way too hot. I felt too ill to care whether Mom was right about Wobbly in the first place.

I didn't know what time it was when Dad finally came up to the cabin to see why I hadn't gone down to see Kenai. Fog seemed to be swirling around me. Then Dad's face suddenly appeared clearly in the middle of it. "Daddy," I whispered, "I feel sick. I want to go home." What a relief to know he was there to take care of me and keep the fire going!

Dad made me some hot tea and bundled me into all the blankets and sleeping bags in the cabin. He carried me out to the little dogsled and tucked me into it. Then he stood on the runners and guided the sled down the trail. I guess Wobbly and the dogs ran along behind us. When we arrived at the Snuggery he carried me in and put me on the couch and told Mom, "She has the flu or an infection. I don't know how it could be the flu because she hasn't been exposed to anything here on the island. So we'll start her on the antibiotics Dr. Towner gave us."

Mom gave me aspirin and the antibiotic. She pulled her rocker up beside me and rubbed my back and legs and sang to me. It felt so good to have her take care of me, like I was a little girl again. In the warm cabin, listening to Mom sing, "Hush, little baby, don't say a word, Papa's gonna buy you a mockin' bird," I finally fell asleep.

Apparently I did have some kind of infection, because by the next morning I felt much better. Dad went up to Long Jake's cabin and brought my schoolbooks and other things down. I didn't say, "I want to stay here now," and Mom and Dad didn't ask me, but they seemed to know that I was ready to be at home again. Wobbly stayed in the barn.

That evening when we sat down to dinner, Mom said,

"Melanie, I'm really glad to have you back with us again. Mealtimes were pretty quiet and stark without your smiling face and chatter."

"It got pretty quiet in Long Jake's cabin, too," I admitted. "At first I really enjoyed the solitude, and I could talk to Wobbly and the dogs, but after a few days, I wished for someone who could respond. I can't imagine how Long Jake lived here alone for all those years without anyone to talk with."

"He talked to the birds and the goats and the voles, and probably imagined that they talked back, but you know he lost the art of conversation until you started visiting him, Mel," Dad smiled at me.

"And then he began to make up for lost time," I laughed. "He used to talk and talk and all I had to do was listen."

"That last winter must have been the most lonely one for him, after he'd had someone to listen to him during the summer," I said. Mom handed me some cranberry relish to eat with my salmon pattie. "You know, when we started out this year I believed that I really needed solitude, and that I could always live in a situation like this," I continued. "But I find I need the two of you for feedback and emotional and spiritual support. More and more I believe we need other people in our lives. It puts a big burden on the two of you to have to respond to my needs all the time. It helped to have people here over Christmas, to soften the intensity of our relationships."

"No man is an island," Dad quoted softly, "and no family is an island either, even if they live on an island by themselves for a winter. We have a great need to communicate. Even Long Jake wrote books for other people to read."

That reminded me of something. "Oh, Mom and Dad, you know what Wobbly did? She chewed up Long Jake's book about kittiwakes! You can still read it but the book is ruined. It makes me feel just sick! Anyway, I hate to admit it, Mom, but you were right. I guess Wobbly does belong in the barn."

"I'm sorry the book was ruined, Melanie. Maybe we can rebind it."

"But it will never be the same. And all because I was so stubborn. Still, I'm glad I went up there to stay for two weeks. It helped me to know what it was like for Long Jake, and to know that I need to be around you two and other people. Thank you for giving me that chance."

Chapter Eight

THE DAYS GREW noticeably longer as February gave way to March. The sun rose again over the inlet in a glorious display of color. It rose high enough to shine on the house all day long, and set splendidly into the rugged mountains on the mainland. But we didn't see it all that often because March came in like a lion, with several violent storms. It seemed like one storm after another rolled up the inlet from out in the Aleutian Islands with howling winds and tons of snow. Huge waves full of ice floes crashed into the shore.

In the mornings all three of us went out with shovels to dig a path through the drifts to the barn. We wore heavy clothes and worked hard, but the wind tore right through our coats and we were all shivering by the time we got safely back into the house. I was glad for the tight barn for

Kenai and I appreciated our snug, cozy house.

It seemed like spring should be coming. Instead, winter howled all the harder around our door. I felt discouraged and blue. I could hardly get up in the morning and drag myself down the stairs, much less work on my schoolwork enthusiastically. Dad and Mom spent a lot of their writing time staring into space, too. We were short with each other, but we didn't yell as much as before I went up to Long Jake's cabin. We were just too depressed to care. If it hadn't been for those occasional sunny days I think we might all have just given up and stayed in bed.

Just when I thought I couldn't stand any more wind, I woke up to silence and the reflection of the pink and orange sky shining on the wall above my bed. I popped out of bed singing, dressed quickly in the cold, and hurried downstairs to help with breakfast. Dad was up, looking chipper, too, but Mom was still in bed.

"Annie's not feeling well this morning," Dad answered my questioning look. "She has pain in her abdomen, so she thought she'd just stay in bed for a while."

"Mom is staying in bed? She must feel really sick!"

"Well, yes, I think she does. She has mentioned having a little pain for several days now, but she thought it was just a passing thing."

After breakfast I took Mom some tea and toast, but she said she wasn't hungry. She looked pale and her face was rigid with pain. Dad started giving her aspirin and antibiotics, but they didn't seem to help much. She stayed in bed the whole day. It was cold up in her bedroom, but she didn't have the strength to come down the stairs to the couch. The house felt very quiet and pale without Mom in it, even though the sun shone grandly through the windows. I moped over my schoolwork. After lunch I took

Kenai for a walk along the beach all the way around the point. Usually it would have been an exciting excursion, but that day I just did it to make the time go by.

By evening Mom's pain was so bad that she lay curled up in her bed. I could hardly stand to see her. She squeezed her eyes tight shut but tears oozed out and she kept moving her hands and feet as if that would help. Dad's face was strained and he was very quiet. At six o'clock he started the generator to charge up the CB battery. He let it charge for two hours, then he started calling out on the CB. It wasn't Grandpa's usual time to listen for us, so he had to call anyone who was listening. Finally someone in Soldotna on the Kenai Peninsula answered, and Dad asked them to call Grandpa and ask him to get on his CB. Soon Dad was talking very seriously to Grandpa explaining Mom's symptoms. Grandpa called the doctor, then came back on the CB. "The doctor says to continue to give her the antibiotic and aspirin, but he says if she has shown no improvement by morning you'd better get a Medivac helicopter to pick her up and take her to the hospital. Charlie, we'll stand by here all night. We'll leave the CB on and if you call one of us will wake up and answer. And tell Anne we're praying!"

Dad switched off the CB and sat for a moment with his head in his hands.

"Dad, if Mom has to go to the hospital tomorrow I think you'd better go with her. I can stay here and look after the animals by myself."

"Oh, I think I would probably stay here with you, honey. Grandma and Grandpa will go to the hospital to be with Annie, so she won't be alone. But I believe she should feel a little better in the morning. The antibiotic should take effect soon. Why don't you get some sleep now." Dad

125

hugged me tight as he kissed me good-night and I didn't even mind. "Don't forget to pray."

"Oh, Daddy, I've been praying all day."

It was hard to go to sleep, but I was so tired from my concern all day that at last I slept restlessly. Dad woke me up very early. "Melanie, please get up and get dressed and stay with Annie while I go down to use the radio. I'm going to call Medivac. I've decided to go out with her and I want you to go too. I'll get your grandpa or Uncle Kent to come and stay with the animals. Annie is much worse."

"But, Dad, what if something happened that Grandpa or Kent couldn't get here? I think you should go with Mom and leave me here. Then when they come I could go over on that helicopter. I just couldn't leave Kenai and the dogs and goats here alone."

"Well, we'll see. But I think your mother needs us with her."

Mom was burning with fever and she didn't seem to be aware of me. I rubbed her down with alcohol while Dad called Grandpa on the radio and asked him to send the Medivac helicopter. Soon he came back upstairs. "Grandpa is going to make arrangements to come over by helicopter this afternoon," he told me, "so I want you to get ready to go across on that helicopter. Then if something should happen you'll be here to take care of things. But there is no reason why Grandpa wouldn't make it."

We didn't try to move Mom since the medics would have a stretcher to carry her. Daddy went down to the beach to mark the place for the copter to land. I held her hand and told her how much I loved her and that I would be praying for her constantly. She squeezed my hand back. Then I heard the big whirring helicopter and things began to move very fast.

126

The doctor and nurse jumped out of the helicopter as soon as it touched the ground, bending over under the still whirring blades. They ran behind Daddy up to the house and right up the stairs, where they bent over Mom and began to check her pulse, her blood pressure, and so forth. I felt shoved out of the way. Daddy stood at the foot of the bed and answered questions. I felt like a little girl again and wished I could stand beside him and hold his hand. The doctor poked at Mom's abdomen and she moaned. "I suspect we've got acute appendicitis here," the doctor told Daddy. "I'll call ahead and have them prepare for surgery as soon as we arrive. Are you going with us, Mr. LaRue? What about your daughter?" He glanced at me.

Dad explained the plans. The pilot came toward the house carrying the stretcher, and Dad sent me down to show him the way. Gently all four of the grown-ups lifted Mom onto the stretcher and the nurse tucked warm blankets around her. The doctor had given her a shot of a painkiller and Mom was drifting off to sleep. I was glad because she looked more peaceful as I whispered good-bye, but I couldn't tell if she heard me.

I walked out to the helicopter beside Daddy who was helping to carry the stretcher. He put his free arm around my shoulder and held tight. As he helped put Mom into the helicopter the nurse said to me, "Your mom ought to be doing just fine by the time you get to Soldotna this afternoon, so don't worry. She's in good hands."

But it was all I could do to keep the tears back as Dad hugged me and kissed me. "She's going to be all right now," he said, "but don't stop praying." He hurried into the helicopter as the blades started whirring and I backed away, waving. Quickly the big bird lifted off the ground, circled once to gain altitude, and headed into the northeast. The tears came. I stood watching until I couldn't hear the faintest hum anymore. As I turned back up the beach to go feed the animals I realized that the wind was blowing in my face, hard. I looked up. The sun was covered with clouds. Big dark clouds were blowing up the inlet. "Here comes another storm," I thought. "I hope it waits until Grandpa gets here."

The wind continued rising as I fed the animals. When I walked back toward the house a few snowflakes drifted by. By now the big helicopter would have arrived in Soldotna, and Mom was probably going to the hospital in an ambulance. . . .

The house felt very empty and quiet. I put wood on the fire in the living area and forced myself to sit down at my desk to do schoolwork. It was the first time all year, except at Jake's cabin, that I tried to have school without Mom at her typewriter on one side and Dad studying or writing on the other. I couldn't concentrate. I got up and brewed a cup of tea. I stood at the window watching the tops blowing off the waves in sprays of white foam and the breakers rolling in on the flood tide. Each wave surged in toward the beach, curled over on itself, and broke against the gravel in a paroxysm of boiling tan lace. Out over the inlet the sky darkened and lowered, gusts of snow blew against the house, and I knew that Grandpa would not be coming in the afternoon. I turned on the CB to see if he would try to call me, but the storm played havoc with the reception. All I could hear was static. Usually when it stormed Dad couldn't get through to Grandpa even at their regularly scheduled contact time, so I was not surprised.

I felt safe and warm in our little house, but lonely and adrift. I felt aimless; I couldn't settle down to doing anything. K.C. curled around my legs and complained. He felt lonely, too. I brought Talkeetna and Goofus inside to keep us company. They lay down and acted like they, too, felt insecure without Mom and Dad. "It's one thing to stay alone at Long Jake's cabin," I thought, "and another to be on the island *all* alone, with no one to talk to or to count on looking after you." I examined all the books on my shelves, and finally settled down to read Madeleine L'Engle's *The Time Trilogy* for the fourth time. With the storm beating against the walls and windows I soon became totally involved with Meg as she searched for her father in outer space.

The next time I looked up and out the window the snow was so thick I couldn't see across the cove. It was nearly noon and the tide was high. I stood at the window and thought, "This is a really high tide. In this weather I'd better keep an eye on the skiffs." Our two boats were pulled up the beach below the fishing cabin and turned over there. They were above the high tide line, but large waves could reach them. The waves carried big chunks of ice in to shore and flung them onto the beach, but everything appeared to be safe. I fixed myself a small bowl of noodles and ate them with Parmesan cheese and some fried Spam and canned apricots. Then I took the dogs out into the blinding snow and returned to *A Wrinkle in Time*.

Every once in a while the thought of Mom pierced my thoughts like a dart, and tears welled up in my eyes. But there wasn't anything I could do except pray. There wasn't anything I could do about being all alone on the island, either, the only person for miles and miles in a terrible storm. I hoped Dad and Grandpa and Grandma wouldn't worry about me, and that they wouldn't even tell Mom that I was alone.

When the light began to fade I bundled up in my down

coat and big boots, pulled on cap and gloves, wrapped a scarf around my face, and went out to look after the animals. It was a struggle to carry more snow in to be melted in the water barrel. During storms Dad and I always did it together. Kenai and the goats were restless in the storm, but Isabella stood fairly quietly while I milked her and fed some of the milk to Wobbly. The chickens huddled against the wall toward the kerosene heater. I brushed Kenai and talked to him quietly. He leaned his long nose against my shoulder and snuffled into my scarf, whispering words of encouragement in horse language. I scratched Wobbly's head around the places where her little horns were growing. She always followed me around the barn while I did the chores. It made me feel needed and special.

I fed the dogs inside their houses, which were deeply covered with snowdrifts. "I'll have a big shoveling job in the morning," I thought as I made my way through the drifts to the woodpile. I carried several armloads of split wood into the porch, although there was already plenty there. The snow seemed to have come alive; it swirled around me in malevolent gusts, howling and shrieking. I couldn't tell how much of it was falling out of the air and how much was coming off the ground. It was good to get back into the warm house again. K.C. purred with relief.

I lit the lantern and cooked my dinner. While I ate I finished *A Wrinkle in Time*. If Meg could go back to Camasotz alone to get Charles Wallace, I could stay alone on a familiar island right here on earth. But I wished I knew if Mom was okay. I turned on the CB again and left it on for an hour and a half. I even tried to contact Grandpa. But the reception was wiped out. Then I figured Daddy would surely send me a message on the regular radio station "bushline," a message program for isolated people without phones. But the radio was full of static, too, and I could barely hear the Kenai station, which was closest, much less Homer or Anchorage stations. The Kenai station didn't have a "bushline."

So I went to bed early without knowing how my mother was, or even if they had safely arrived in Soldotna. It was hard to go to sleep, but Dad had waked me up very early in the morning and I was tired. K.C. curled against my back and felt warm. I finally fell asleep.

I woke up out of a long dream and I couldn't tell where the dream stopped and reality began because the storm in my dream was a real storm. The wind was howling more fiercely than I had ever heard it before. It was blowing out of the northeast now. I could picture it boiling up in the Chugach Mountains east of Anchorage and leaping ferociously down over the inlet toward Gresham Island. Beyond the howl of the wind, though, I heard waves breaking, and they sounded like they were almost up to the house.

I wrapped a blanket around myself and went to the window and looked out into the pale dark. The tide was very high. "It must be about 1:00 in the morning," I reflected, remembering when high tide was during the day. But the tide was now being blown in on gigantic waves, far bigger than we had ever seen here in our cove. They must have been ten footers slamming into the beach with huge chunks of ice in them.

Crash, crash, crash, one after the other the waves piled in and the thud of the ice seemed almost to shake the house. "The skiffs! Oh, my goodness, they've probably been washed away! Or crushed by an ice floe." I tried to think what to do. Well, Dad would say that I was more important than the boats, and I didn't think it was safe for me

131

to go out into the night alone. I would have to wait until morning and see if there was anything left for me to do something about. So I crawled back into bed, but I didn't sleep well the rest of the night. The wind roared and shook the house, the waves crashed. I was glad when the tide began to ebb and the waves receded with it.

In the morning the storm showed no signs of letting up, but the tide was out and after I fed the animals I trudged down the beach between chunks of ice to see how the boats had fared. The waves had eaten away at the beach so there was a gravelly bank at the high tide line. They had washed the gravel out from under the sterns of the boats, but fortunately no ice had fallen right on the hulls. I knew I had to get the boats further up the beach because the afternoon tide would be even higher than the nighttime one, and the waves probably at least as big. Of course, I couldn't budge the boats by myself. I had to have Kenai to help. But even with Kenai, there had always been several strong people pushing on the boat to help him get it started. And the boats had always been turned right side up, sliding along the beach on their keels, when Kenai had pulled them. I wasn't at all sure he and I could do this job alone. But we would try.

I went back to the barn and shoveled snow away from the barnyard door, to the gate, and beyond it to the path between the house and barn. It took me probably an hour and a half to do that and I was so drenched with sweat inside my coat that I had to go indoors and change clothes. I drank a cup of tea and ate a couple of cookies. Then I took the shovel down to the boats and cleared the snow away from them. The snow was icy and hard but it wasn't very deep because the wind kept the beach pretty well scoured. I made a place for Kenai to pull them further up the beach.

Meanwhile the tide was on the flood and the waves were piling higher and higher and closer and closer. I had to hurry. Finally I harnessed Kenai. He was excited about getting to go out, but when I led him through the barn door into the swirling snow he wanted to turn right around and go back inside. Somehow I persuaded him to go with me. We had to walk slowly and carefully because the rocks on the beach were icy.

I fastened the bowline of the yellow boat to Kenai's harness. I went to his head and quietly told him what I wanted him to do. "Now pull, Kenai!" He lunged forward, head down. Nothing happened. "Pull again, try it again, boy." Again he pulled. I hated to leave him alone because he didn't like the snow blowing in his face or the sound of the waves crashing behind him, but I thought maybe if I pushed on the stern while Kenai pulled, we could break the boat loose. So I explained to him what I was going to do and hurried to the stern. It was icy and hard to get a grip. "Pull, Kenai!" I yelled, pushing with all my might.

Suddenly the boat broke loose. I was pushing so hard I fell right on my face as Kenai pulled it away from me. Quickly I jumped up and ran to his head as he continued to strain and pull. We stopped to rest several times before we had the boat well up out of reach of the waves. In fact it was almost even with the front of the fishing cabin. We followed the same procedure to pull up the other boat. "Oh, Kenai, you good horse!" I hugged him. "We saved the boats for Daddy and he will be so glad."

Kenai was wet from sweat and snow so we hurried back to the barn. The unheated barn felt warm compared with the wind-driven air outdoors. I rubbed him down until he was dry, the whole time telling him what a good horse he was. The goats gathered against their side of the stall to hear what had happened and I told them all about it.

By the time I was finished with Kenai, it was past lunchtime and I felt starved. The tide was almost high and again the waves were immense. I ate my lunch at Dad's desk, where I could watch them curl in over the beach and break in a horrendous explosion of water. I watched a wave hurl a table-sized chunk of ice up on the beach and wondered how the boats had ever survived last night. What a relief to know they were safe! Now if only I knew my mother was feeling much better I would feel pretty good. But I could pray about that and trust. I couldn't let my mind even consider anything else. I gave up on my schoolwork and started reading *A Wind in the Door*. Outdoors the wind bellowed and wailed, the snow scoured the roof, walls, and windows, and the waves slammed into shore in endless rhythm. Indoors I was snug and warm with k.c. curled up on my lap, a cup of tea on the table beside me, and Meg and Proginoskes for companions.

Too soon it was time for chores and then dinner. I was so tired my whole body ached. I went to bed early. That night I slept the night through. I woke up to peace. The storm was over. The wind still blew but it was a breeze compared to the day before. Light clouds scudded across the sky and in the east the sun promised to break through them before long. Out in the inlet the waves were now long swells. I dressed and hurried downstairs to turn on the CB radio. It was still a little static-y but not bad. As I broke an egg to fry I heard Grandpa's familiar voice:

"Snuggery, Snuggery, this is Cottonwood Cache. Snuggery, are you there?"

Oh, my own dear Grandpa! "Cottonwood Cache, Snuggery. Hi, Grandpa, how is my mom?"

"Snuggery, Cottonwood Cache. Hello, Melanie. It sure

is good to hear your voice and know you made it through the storm. Your mother is doing fine. She had appendicitis, and she had surgery as soon as she arrived in Soldotna. She is feeling much better already. Your parents are terribly eager to hear how you are doing."

"Cottonwood Cache, Snuggery. Oh, I'm fine, and so are all the animals. That was the worst storm we've ever had. I'm sure glad it waited until Mom got safely to the hospital. Grandpa, are you going to come to the island when the weather is good enough? And when are Mom and Dad coming back?"

"Snuggery, Cottonwood Cache. Your Mom will probably be out of the hospital tomorrow, so your dad will be returning to the island today or tomorrow. Anne will stay with us for a week or so until the doctor says she's well enough to return. Charlie says to tell you if you want to come over on the return flight when he goes, you may. We'd love to see you!"

"Cottonwood Cache, Snuggery. I'd love to see you, too, Grandpa, but since I've been here this long I think I'll just stay here until summer. Besides I'd hate for Dad to have to be alone here that long. Please tell Mom and Dad that I love them and I'm so glad Mom is better."

"Snuggery, Cottonwood Cache. I sort of guessed you would want to stay over there. I suspect your dad will wait until tomorrow to go to the island so why don't you plan to talk to me again at 7:00 this evening? I don't want to talk too long now or you'll use up your battery. So this will be Cottonwood Cache over and out."

"Cottonwood Cache, Snuggery. Okay, Grandpa, I'll listen for you at seven. Tell Dad I'll be watching for him." I could hardly stand to end the conversation. "This is Snuggery clear."

"Cottonwood Cache clear."

I switched off the CB and felt lonely again. But I was relieved to know Mom was fine and getting better. "I sure wish Dad would come today," I thought as I fixed my breakfast. "I think I'll bake bread this morning in case he comes."

After I fed the animals and carried snow in to melt in the water barrels in both the house and the barn, I started the bread. The sun broke through the clouds and shone in the window as I turned the bread out on the table to knead. The bright sun lightened my spirit; kneading the bread in rhythm calmed me. I felt capable of handling whatever situation might arise before Dad came home. When the bread was kneaded I put it in the bowl to rise and dusted and swept the house. I went outdoors into the bright sunshine—it reflected on the fresh white snow blindingly—and dug open the path to the barn. I let the dogs loose and they romped happily in the snowdrifts. Talkie dug her nose into the snow and tossed it in the air. Snow clung to her nose and eyelashes and she looked so comical I rolled in the snow with laughter. I let Wobbly out, too; she tried to follow the dogs into the deep snow, but had to be rescued frequently.

When the path was open I took Kenai for a walk down the beach. What a contrast from the day before when we could hardly see where we were going and enormous waves pounded the shore, driven by the fierce wind. Today the sun shone in a wide blue sky. I could see the Chigmit Mountains across the channel, all white and steep with blue and purple shadows marking each steep ridge and every deep canyon. The island itself rose from the water in gentle billows of snow, punctuated by stands of dark green spruce trees and gaunt gray cottonwoods. Across the inlet I could see the distant Kenai Mountains. The deep blue water rolled in to the beach in long rhythmic swells. Huge gray chunks of ice littered the beach along the high tide line and above it. A large floe lay on the spot where the yellow skiff had been before Kenai pulled it up. If we hadn't moved it that boat would have a big hole in the hull! Good for Kenai!

I was just taking the fragrant loaves of bread out of the oven in the late afternoon when I heard a distant hum. I had been listening so hard for that sound that I imagined it all afternoon, so this time I waited until I was sure it was a helicopter before I ran out to greet it. Sure enough, a whirlybird much smaller than the Medivac helicopter came chattering across the channel. Daddy! I jumped up and down and waved as they circled over the cabin and then landed on the beach. In a minute I was in a great big warm hug and I didn't think Dad would ever let me go. Well, to tell the truth, I didn't want to let him go either. But the pilot was eager to return to Kenai before sunset, so Dad quickly helped him unload a couple of boxes and we watched him whirl away. As the noise faded in the distance and we turned to walk back up to the house, Dad looked over at me.

"You're sure everything is okay? I could hardly stand it when I realized the weather was too bad for your grandpa to come over. I had no intention of leaving you here alone for more than a few hours, especially in a storm.

"Well, I survived! We all did fine. But I'm so glad to have you back! And that Mom's okay; tell me all about her."

"Well, she really wanted to come along home to you. When we told her that you were here alone she almost came unglued. Well, I should say unstitched, because she had her appendix removed as soon as we arrived in Soldotna. It was so swollen the doctor was surprised it hadn't burst. So we were really thankful we hadn't waited any longer to get her out. She would have been much sicker if that had happened. But she is feeling a lot better already and Grandpa and Grandma are with her today. She said that she would heal up much faster if she knew that I was here with you, so I came as soon as I could."

We reached the house and took the boxes inside. As we unpacked fresh vegetables and fruit—my mouth watered!—I told Dad all about my own adventures. He was amazed that Kenai and I had been able to move the boats all alone. "They were frozen in solid and upside down. I just don't see how you did it!" Dad must have said that three times. "Thank you! It would have been a real problem to have a new boat built in time to fish in it this summer, and we couldn't really afford it. You were taking a real risk with Kenai. He could have slipped and fallen and been hurt."

"Oh, he's a surefooted guy, Dad," I smiled with satisfaction. "You know he's a special horse. He knew what he had to do and he did it."

"Oh, yes, he's a special horse, all right. He belongs to a very special girl! Melanie, you don't know how proud I am of you. I had every confidence that you could manage in the storm."

"Well, I did manage," I said. "But I sure didn't feel very confident that stormy night and day. I hope I never have to do it again." I bit into a crisp, sweet apple.

We had a wonderful tossed salad, fresh bread, and pork chops for dinner. What a feast! I felt warm and secure and loved as I climbed into bed that night and k.c. settled in against my back.

Chapter Nine

IT'S FUNNY HOW YOU can be so irritated and annoyed by someone, but when they are gone you miss them terribly. While my Mom was gone, I forgot all about how she sang la-tada-la-la to familiar tunes when she couldn't think of the words, or how she stared out the window when I thought she should be writing, or how she wanted to hug me when I didn't want to be touched. In fact, I could have used a nice hug from her.

Even with Dad there, the house seemed empty and cold and depressing. Mom usually has a smile and an optimistic attitude even though she does worry a lot about safety. She keeps things picked up, lights candles, puts plants or shells or pieces of driftwood in just the right arrangement, and cooks special foods that Dad and I like. She does all this stuff because she loves us, and I had forgotten that over the long winter of being so close together. What I missed most was the warm blanket of love that she wraps around us, the sunshine of love that usually fills the house when she is there.

So Dad and I felt lonely and kind of at loose ends during the week when Mom was gone. We talked to her every night on the CB and that helped, and we had good times working together outdoors in the late March sunshine, but what a relief it was when she arrived home. The beach was clear enough that Uncle Kent brought her in his little Champ at low tide. I felt like a little kid, dancing around with excitement as the little plane slowed to a stop. Uncle Kent picked me up and swung me around as though I *were* a little kid. When he set me down he said, "You are getting so big and grown-up I don't know if I can turn you upside down anymore, Melanie. Besides I hear you're a heroine, rescuing boats out of the teeth of the storm, and heroines are very dignified, I understand."

"Oh, I'm not a heroine, Uncle Kent, and I'm not dignified, and I'll never be too grown-up to be turned upside down." I ducked into the bear hug that Dad was giving Mom. "Oh, Mom, I'm so glad you're back. I really missed you!"

"I missed you, too, Melanie. And I'm awfully glad to be home."

"Are you feeling okay now, Mom? Are you back to normal?"

"Well, I still get tired easily and I'll need to rest a lot and not do anything strenuous for a while, but I feel a hundred percent better than I did. How is Wobbly?"

I'm always surprised that Mom really does care about my animals, even though she doesn't want goats in the house and she won't touch hamsters, and so forth. So I told

140

her about how Wobbly and everyone else was doing as we walked slowly up to the house.

Uncle Kent stayed until the tide began to flood again; then he took off with a promise to come back some weekend soon. He told us that he couldn't fish with us the coming summer because his business as an airplane mechanic was growing and he had to nurture it along over the summer. But Aunt Rose planned to come back, and Dad said I was capable of helping him fish myself. We wouldn't need another person.

"Oh, Dad, do you really think I'm strong enough?" I asked him.

"Anyone who could take care of the livestock, look after the fire, haul snow to melt for water, shovel snow, *and* move two skiffs up the beach in a blizzard is someone I want for a fishing partner any day," Dad assured me. "Anyone with the good judgment to manage all those things all by herself on an isolated island, has the judgment needed to be a full-fledged fisherperson."

"Thank you, Daddy," I smiled. I still thought of myself as a little girl who couldn't do everything, or if she did, did it to spite her parents. It was hard to imagine myself as nearly grown up, responsible for helping to run a fishing site. "But that's what this year has been good for," I thought, as I mulled over our conversation later. "I have learned to be independent and responsible. I've learned to discipline myself." I was quite amazed.

The days lengthened through April and the sun climbed higher and higher in the sky each day. The snow got soft and slushy and melted all over the place. The barnyard turned into a mud swamp that came halfway up my kneeboots when I led Kenai through it for our rides on the beach. We let the goats out to meander along behind us.

There was still nothing green for them to munch on, but they enjoyed the fresh air and sunshine. We all did. In spite of the wet snow, we spent as much time as possible outdoors in the clean, bright air. The waterfall ran again by the end of April, so we no longer had to cut snow blocks every day. Instead we hitched Kenai to the cart and hauled tanks of icy cold water back from the waterfall every two or three days.

By May the ground was bare in some places, especially on the point. The woods came to life with bird song. Little green Wilson's warblers and yellow warblers, brown streaked sparrows, robins and varied thrushes, chickadees and redpolls and pine grosbeaks flitted through the branches. A big hawk, the northern harrier, began to make regular evening forays over the point. He flew low over the bare ground, searching for voles and other small creatures. Eider ducks, flashy black and white drakes and dull brown females, and old squaw ducks with long thin tails congregated in the cove. I collected eider down from among the rocks where the fat ducks basked in the sun. Flocks of geese flew over the point on their way further north to their nesting grounds. I love to hear their joyful, chaotic honking. It always sounds like a song of wanderlust to me.

The wanderlust song made me realize how long I had been living in one place, on one end of a small island, for eight months. I thought again about my friends in Anchorage, excited about the last days of school, worrying over final exams. I thought about how much fun it would be to take the train up to Denali National Park or to Whittier, or to drive down the Kenai Peninsula to Homer as we often did in the spring. I looked forward to the arrival of Aunt Rose and the other fishermen on the island. "What do Rob and Jim Hanson look like by now? Won't it be fun to have boat races and picnics on the beach and to sing together with the guitar?"

The alders and cottonwoods turned red and then green as their leaves popped open almost overnight. New grass and fireweed shoots poked up through the tangled brown dead grasses from previous years. In the woods fiddleheads grew in thick clumps. They pushed up out of the ground and shed their brown tissue skins as they grew taller and uncurled into green fern fronds. Broad devil's club leaves unfurled, dwarf dogwood and tiny starflowers replaced the snow. On the point I found the dull brown bells of chocolate lilies, tight spikes of lupine buds, the unique leaves of the wild geranium.

During a week of extreme tides in late May we sanded and fiberglassed the worn spots on the hulls of the skiffs, then turned them over and let Kenai pull them down below the high tide line. We put out the running line and a buoy, and when the boats floated we tied them out on the lines. It felt good to see the boats floating there, as though we were no longer so isolated.

"Dad, let's dig clams at low tide this evening and then find a place over there to cook and eat them with a picnic. Could we?"

"That sounds like a great idea, Melanie. Why don't you go get the food ready and I'll find the clam shovels and buckets and things?"

"I can't think of anything I'd rather do," Mom agreed.

It was a sunny, calm day. With an extra motor in the boat, buckets, shovels, picnic goodies, warm coats for the late evening chill, and both dogs, we headed out over the water to the sandbar at the mouth of the river. As the water got shallow I jumped out in my hip boots and walked the boat as close as I could to the sandbar. Then I tied an anchor to the bowline and carried it up on the bar. The dogs jumped out into the water and splashed to the shore. They ran and played on the broad open sandbar while Mom, Dad, and I dug clams. We took turns digging with the small shovels and reaching down to catch the elusive clam as it tried to siphon itself down out of reach. In no time at all we had half a bucket of clams, which was more than enough for our picnic.

The tide had just turned as we splashed back to the boat. I took up the anchor and Dad and I pushed the boat out to where it was deep enough to put the motor down. Then we headed for the beach close to where we had gotten wood in the fall. While the dogs romped on the beach and finally lay down panting, we gathered wood, built a fire, and cleaned the clams. Mom put out bread, a salad made of canned peas and cheese with onions and mayonnaise, sliced potatoes ready to be fried, and canned fruit and cookies. Dad fried the clams quickly in the frying pan over the open fire. Mmmmm, they were good, so tender they slid right down my throat. Then he fried the potatoes. We sat on logs around the fire and ate until we felt satisfied. The sun still hung high in the sky over the triple peaks of Mt. Illiamna, to the west of the island and south of us. Gulls floated in the water or stalked on the beach close to us, hoping for some discarded clams.

The water lay calm and slaty blue all the way to Gresham Island, all green and still in the sunshine, with snow still on the upper ridges and pointing down the gullies. "Isn't it a beautiful island?" I asked no one in particular. "I'm glad we lived there. I learned a lot."

"What did you learn?" Dad asked.

"Well, I learned to be responsible, to do my part so that things go well for all of us. I learned to discipline myself, to

144

study hard so I would have time for other things, to look after my animals when they needed it instead of when I felt like it. I found out that I am a basically independent person, but that I need other people around. I needed you and Mom to talk to, to help me get through depressed times, to share excitement with and beauty, like this evening, and to encourage me when I make mistakes or try something new. I couldn't live all alone, like Long Jake did, but I do need a lot of space. I would have a hard time living in a crowded city, or being surrounded by too many people. Some people need lots of other people around and that's good, but I don't and that's good, too."

We sat quietly for a while, gazing out toward the island across the water. Then Dad asked, "What did you learn, Annie?"

"Well," Mom thought for a minute, "I learned not to worry so much or be so fearful of every little thing that might possibly happen. I guess I learned to be more dependent on God's faithfulness. I learned that I can get a lot of writing done in isolation, as I had always thought, but I also learned during the week in Homer after my surgery that I need feedback and encouragement from other people, too. A book that will touch other people's lives must draw on life and the things that happen to people every day. I find that my desire to be away from obligations is selfish and not the best thing for me. I want to respond to other people's needs with love and compassion, not as an obligation but by choice, in order to be a whole person. But it's something that requires effort on my part."

"What about you, Dad?" I asked after Mom's voice faded behind the lap of water and the grunting of the seagulls.

"One thing I learned was the obvious," Dad mused.

"We can function independently up to a certain point, but we always turn out to be dependent on other people. For instance, the Medivac team and Grandpa on the CB, not to mention the helicopter pilots and the tender that brought our supplies last summer. We were more dependent than we knew on a lot of people's prayers. I learned that I can write, although we'll have to wait to see if others agree with that and my book gets published. But the most important thing for me is that I like to have a lot of people around. I really like to be up to my ears in challenging work with colleagues and employees. I didn't realize how important that was to me or how much I would miss it until this year. I could interact with the two of you . . . ."

"And you did," Mom interrupted.

". . . but you are both pretty independent. In spite of what you've said you seemed to thrive on isolation or else your avenues for reaching out—writing and caring for animals—are different from mine. I like to be in a situation where I can interact with people directly, where they actually depend on me for something. Then I feel I'm making a contribution."

"No man is an island, entire of itself," Mom quoted John Donne again. "Every man is a piece of the continent, a part of the main . . . ."

I gazed at Gresham Island, separated from the mainland by the channel, but connected to it by the sea floor underneath the channel. "That's the way I'd like to live, with some space around me, like an island, but connected to the mainland, aware of the pulse of the whole universe around me and being a part of it. Oh, I can't explain it." I stopped, frustrated.

"I think I know what you mean," Dad replied, softly. "I suspect we all have our own inner island where we are

146

alone, no matter where we are or who is with us, but it is in that place, somehow, that we are most a part of the whole creation...." His voice trailed off, and we sat on the logs together in silence for a long time. The dogs lay at our feet, curled up and sleeping. A flock of white-winged scoters flew in a long straight line just above the surface of the water, wings beating in unison. In the woods behind us a confusion of bird songs filled the quiet, swallows swooped and darted in the air above the beach.

Sitting there with my parents on either side of me and the whole earth around me, I knew that I was a part of it all, a part of something much bigger than I was, so grand I couldn't imagine it, yet special and important as myself, Melanie. "Joy," I thought, "this is what joy is."

The sky turned pink and lavender as the sun dropped behind the mountains. The air turned chilly. We packed the picnic things together and put them in the boat, then headed out across the water toward Gresham Island, leaving a long wake behind us.

GUENN MARTIN is a writer, secretary, commercial fisherwoman, and graduate student who lives in Atlanta, Georgia, where she moved recently after living in Anchorage, Alaska for 10 years. She was born in Lancaster, Pennsylvania, spent her early teenage years in a small Eskimo village in western Alaska, and graduated in 1966 from Goshen College, Goshen, Indiana, with a B.A. in English. Following completion of a two-year apprenticeship as a psychological assistant, she worked in the area of child psychology, particularly with autistic children. She is study for a graduate degree in psychology.

Guenn is a member of Anchorage Mennonite Fellowship. She is married to Dr. Clair Martin, a dean at Emory University in Atlanta. Their teenage daughter, Sonja, is also an accomplished fisherwoman and an animal lover who has many pets, ranging from a horse to a boa constrictor.

Guenn enjoys watching birds and feeds huge flocks of them on her deck each winter. She is an avid reader of many types of books. Since 1981, Guenn and her family have operated a commercial salmon fishing business on an island in Cook Inlet during the summer months. She developed her previous book, *Remember the Eagle Day*, as a result of the fishing experience.

Remember the Eagle Day received the C. S. Lewis Silver Honor Medal from *Christian School* magazine (published by the Association of Christian Schools International) as one of the top five children's books of the year with a Christian message. It was selected from about 200 entries.